CA

CA$H OUT 2

ASSA RAYMOND BAKER

GOOD 2 GO PUBLISHING

CASH IN CASH OUT 2

Written by Assa Raymond Baker

Cover Design: Davida Baldwin – Odd Ball Designs

Typesetter: Mychea

ISBN: 9781947340343

Copyright © 2019 Good2Go Publishing

Published 2019 by Good2Go Publishing

7311 W. Glass Lane • Laveen, AZ 85339

www.good2gopublishing.com

https://twitter.com/good2gobooks

G2G@good2gopublishing.com

www.facebook.com/good2gopublishing

www.instagram.com/good2gopublishing

CA$H IN

CA$H OUT 2

PROLOUGE

Bonkerz was hosting two events simultaneously, one a birthday bash for two of the
dancers, and the other a small bachelor party
that Murdah had Scrap throw together for his
friend at the last minute. He also had him bail
out Badman from jail for $30,000 and pay Mike-
Mike $10,000 more to take the charges, since it
was his fault that Badman and Tommy got
busted in the parking lot and went to jail.

The reason why Badman still needed to be
bailed out was because an officer broke her
thumb when she was trying to restrain him

during a physical altercation he had gotten into at Milwaukee County Jail's putrid, filthy, and overcrowded booking room.

Murdah also spent another large sum of money on a lawyer who was hard at work trying to get the battery case dismissed for him. But until then, Badman was out partying it up with his crew at Bonkerz.

Max and Slugga joined the festivities, even though their visit was not for fun. They were just scoping the place out to work out their plans for robbing Scrap, so Champagne could finally make her getaway from him and repay him for how he treated her. Max came up with a new plan because Slugga did not like Champagne knowing all the details of how it would go down.

He enlisted Slugga's help to pull it off because of the changes. Like Max, Slugga needed to see the layout of Bonkerz firsthand, so he could know what they were up against when they made their move. Robbery was not a new activity for him.

Before Slugga met his wife and she birthed the first of his five children, he was a feared stickup kid straight from the mean streets of Chicago's south side. The reason he was coming out of retirement was not because of Max, but because his two oldest children needed his help. He needed extra money to pay for his one son's schooling as well as a good lawyer, so his other son would not spend the rest of his life in prison for a crime he did not commit.

"Hell yeah! This is what I'm talkin' about. Ass and titties! Just ass and titties in every direction I look in this bitch. My nigga, you gonna get me put out."

"Yeah right, Sara ain't letting yo' ass go too far. She might put you on the couch, but not outta the house. And don't blame nothing ya do up in here on me. Yo' ass could've taken my word for it, but, no. You had to check things out fo yo'self. I know the real, bruh. Ya just wanted to have a little fun," Max responded to his friend. "Here, the first rounds on me. Get us some beers and 200 ones so we can chill, and you can get a better feel of the place. I'ma go let Kake know I'm here right quick."

Max pointed at her so Slugga would know where he would be.

"Damn, Max, you don't give that bitch her credit. She ain't no dime, but what she's lacking, she makes up for with all that ass. Damn, my nigga! Damn!"

Slugga noticed Badman at the bar talking to a stripper in a white-and-pink baby doll dress with legs for days.

"I'ma go holla at my nigga Bad over there right quick. Just so you know if I'm not at the table when ya get back."

"Whoa, bruh, you know him? He's one of the niggas I seen the ol' boy we finna hit with, just so ya know," Max warned, not taking his eye off Badman.

"I know, but he don't know what we here for. So, go do what you gotta do, and let me work this how I do."

With that said, the two went their separate ways. Max strolled over to where Kake was grinding erotically in a man's face. He was handing her all of his money, since he did not want what she was doing to end. But when she looked up and saw Max standing there watching her work, she put the lap dance she was in the middle of on hold with a promise to come right back for another song. She told Max that she would not be ready to go for another hour and a half or so.

"Hey, you didn't have to stop yo' money for me. I can wait. Hell, I'm thinkin' I like watchin' ya get down like that. That move ya did on a handstand was hot—on the real."

"That's good to know. If you be a good boy, mama might let you see what it feels like with you inside this kitty tonight," Kake told him before returning to finish her show for the horny client.

While looking for Slugga, Max spotted Champagne in a tense conversation with a tall, scantily-dressed white girl he thought was another dancer. As he made his way over to talk to her, Scrap popped up out of nowhere. But by that time, the two had made eye contact. Champagne whispered something in the other girl's ear that made her head in Max's direction.

"You Max, right?" Playthang asked while

dancing all up on him.

"Yeah, why?"

She took his hand and led him the other way.

"Champ said for you to meet here in the champagne room because she doesn't want Scrap to see her talking to you," she explained as she escorted Max to the VIP room.

Once they were inside, she flipped the in-use switch and then left him there alone. But he did not have to wait long before Champagne joined him in the dimly lit room.

"I can't stay long. Murdah wants me to perform for his guy's party over there. So what's up?"

"It's cool. Me and my nigga are just here checkin' things out. But since I got ya in here, let me put you up on the new plan, 'cause there's too many of them niggas here right now for us to make a move."

"Why? It should be simpler now with 'em all up here, don't you think?" she asked, taking a seat on the loveseat.

"Hell no! You said the punk's office is hooked up to his phone, so as soon as I hit that door, they gonna be on me. Unless you can get his phone."

"Yeah right. Not in here."

"Okay. Since they up here partyin' and shit, that means we got another day to do this before he moves the money again. So how we gonna play it now is, I need ya to stay with him all day tomorrow and keep him off his square until we run up in this bitch."

"Hold up! Y'all gonna rob him with me there?" Champagne replied, looking skeptical of the change in plans.

"Yeah! Like I told you before, I don't want this to fall back on either of us. So, doing it like this, the nigga can't say you got nothing to do with it. I promise you, won't nobody get hurt if everything goes right."

Champagne knew what she had to do in order to ensure things worked out and to be sure they were all in the same place. When she returned to the bachelor party to get Playthang on board to spend the night with her and Scrap, she ran into Badman.

"Say, say, Champ!" he called out as he

stopped her from walking on by. "I know you know. What's up with Nici? Is he still hot at me?" he asked, using Playthang's real name instead of her known moniker.

"Who's Nici and why would I know that?" she asked, unsure if he was talking about her friend.

"Come on, don't act like ya don't know who I'm talkin' about. I know about Playthang. I'm just shocked to see the bitch up in here droppin' it for a pimp." He laughed. "But I just wanna know if the sh-him's still mad at me and shit."

"Don't call her that, and if ya wanna know somethin' about her, go ask her yo'self. I don't know shit that went on between y'all and don't care."

"Does my nigga know what 'that' is you got

around him?" he asked in a devious tone of voice.

"You so fuckin' disrespectful! Play is not a 'that,' and why wouldn't Scrap know who he's fuckin' with," Champagne answered before she marched off in search of her friend.

She was a bit irritated by Badman's questioning, and she planned to tell Scrap about it after she found out what had happened from Playthang.

* * *

Slugga was relieved to be on his way home and away from the temptation to cheat on his wife. He and Max promised to meet back up around ten in the morning before he got behind the wheel of his car and drove home feeling good about the day ahead.

"Do you even know how to drive?" Max asked Kake while sitting in his truck parked behind his house.

"Yeah, I passed my road test and all that good shit. I just don't got my L's 'cause I didn't have the money to pay for 'em at the time, and I've been fuckin' procrastinating with it ever since," she answered, putting out the blunt she was smoking with him and Slugga on the drive from the club.

"On what? Kake, ya need to get on that shit ASAP," Max said as he removed a set of car keys from his keychain and handed them to her. "Here, I'ma let you use my car to get around in. Don't fuck my shit up, Kake!" he warned her while staring into her eyes, which he noticed for the first time were gray.

The other times they were together he thought she was wearing contacts, but now he could see they were her real eye color.

"No, I'm straight, Max, 'cause if somethin' happened to it, I don't got the money to cash out for it, and I don't wanna fuck up shit with you. So, yeah, I'm good," she turned down his offer, handing the keys back to him.

"Look here, ma. If I couldn't afford it, I wouldn't do it. But I'ma need ya to be able to move around how ya want to help me get this loud pack off, if ya down?"

"Is you asking me to sell weed for you, 'cause hell yeah, I'm down. I was just talkin' to my friend about going half with me on a half-pound of loud."

"What friend?" he asked, wanting to know if she was talking about a male or female friend.

"Dysnee. She dances at Bonkerz with me when she's in town. You've seen her before. She's the super-dark-skinned girl with the bright mermaid hair."

"Yeah, I know who ya talkin' about. That bitch calls herself Disney?"

"No, that's her real name. It's spelled different from what ya thinkin' it is. She spells hers D-Y-S-N-E-E. Her stage name is Compton."

Max laughed and said, "HWA! You two can be the new Hoes With Attitudes and shit."

He opened the door to get out, and at the same time spotted two of his hype buddies coming down the alley.

"Come in for a minute. I gotta handle somethin' right quick and get my stuff outta the car before you go."

"Max, this is the first time you had me at yo' house. It's not bad."

"Oh, I'm glad ya like it," he said as he flashed his golden smile.

He then handled his business with the two dope heads and hastily cleaned out the Cruze in one wop.

When he got back inside the house, he gave Kake five ounces of the ten pounds of kush that he planned on having her and Dysnee sell for him.

"Daddy, I'ma run through this real fast, 'cause I won't have to look for it when my folks call lookin' for some. Once I tell everybody I got it, it's on!"

"You do yo' thang. See if ya girl wants to get down, too. Oh, and, Kake, one of them is yours, so you won't be smokin' up my profit and shit."

"That's good lookin', but you don't gotta worry about that. I know how to handle my business before pleasure," she promised as she put the weed inside her bag. "Do ya got a blunt rolled so we can smoke on it?"

Max gave her a Swisher and some weed to roll up. Then they got in a quickie before Kake drove herself home. Max went right to bed, so he would not be tired in a few hours when he and Slugga ran up at Bonkerz. Max lay in bed spending the money before he even had it in his hands. He thought about buying a new car—maybe something foreign and eye-catching. Thoughts raced in his mind as he tossed and turned until he fell asleep.

CHAPTER 1

Anticipation caused the marauders to meet up two hours earlier than they agreed. They ran through the plan a few more times before they found themselves parked in the perfect spot, giving them a full view of Scrap's personal side entrance to his office. After about an hour and a half of sitting in the warm dark blue Journey, cars started to pull into the parking lot of Bonkerz. At that time, Max received a text from Champagne that briefly gave him the rundown on what he and Slugga were witnessing. Her text said that Scrap had a meeting at the club and she would let them know when it was good to make their move.

"Slugga, that's that same damn moving truck that was here the other day that I followed and hit that lick for that loud," Max pointed out when he saw the box truck turn into the lot followed by a Chevy Malibu and an Escalade.

"We should follow that muthafucka when it leaves 'cause that's where all the money is at, on the real."

"Ya know it's whatever with me. I gotta good feeling about today. But I don't want ol' girl to think I'm on some bullshit with her. I done put this lick off twice already," he explained as they watched Scrap walk out of Bonkerz and hand the three Latino men a nice-sized knapsack.

One of the guys took a quick peek inside and

then got back into the Malibu while the others helped load up the Escalade with more television boxes.

"Shit, that's Badman's Audi coming," Slugga informed Max just as the Malibu turned into the lot. "Fuck the truck! Follow the car. We can come back after we get that bag from them fools. I'm not trying to deal with all of them. It's too much for just us. I know that nigga Bad ain't gonna make it easy for us and shit," Slugga told the young thug as they tailed the unsuspecting Malibu.

"So, we hittin' both of these today? Slugga, you's a monster for this shit here!" Max saluted. "How we gonna do this here? Jack 'em in the car, or what?"

"I thought about that but check it. If that was a money pickup, then we need to know where it's going so we can get the rest. I got a good feeling this is them nigga's plug. If so and we pull this off, we gonna be set for real. But be ready to use that burner 'cause it might get rough with these Mexicans."

Max got another text from Champagne saying that Murdah called a meeting in the club, and Scrap sent her home until they were done.

"Well, we just got the window needed to do this. Champ just got sent to the crib 'cause them niggas are having a meeting. So let's get all the way focused and worry about that other shit another day."

"Nope, bro! We gotta do all this shit today.

I'm not tryin' to get back into the habit. I'm too old for this shit!" Slugga told Max as they pulled over and parked down the street from the driveway into which the Malibu turned. "What up? Why you ain't riding past?"

"I'ma walk by just in case they lookin' for us to drive past. Plus, I can peep out mo' shit walkin' than driving. Feel me?" he answered, putting on his baseball cap and stashing his gun under the driver's seat before opening the door.

"Bruh, ya sure you wasn't on this type of shit already and just ain't telling me? 'Cause I would've driven around the block and then walked by back in the day when this was my bread and meat," Slugga said, doing the same as Max did before he also got out of the van.

Max shook his head. "Where ya going?" he asked, upon seeing Slugga start through the gangway.

"Man, I gotta piss like a racehorse," he yelled back over his shoulder as he jogged away.

* * *

Slugga relieved himself between overflowing garbage dumpsters in the alley behind the house in which they parked in front. Slugga noticed an unoccupied cable utility van, which gave him an idea that would help with the home invasion. So he finished up and then did a quick search of the van, taking anything he thought might be useful. Slugga then took the long way back to their van just in case a snooping neighbor saw him and ratted him out.

"Bro, what's all this? What ya get in to?" Max asked once he returned and found him in back of the Journey rummaging through a tool bag and wearing a workman's utility belt.

"This here is how we gonna get in that shot. Here, put this on!" Slugga said as he tossed Max a bright-colored worker's vest and a hard hat. "Muthafuckas don't think twice about opening doors for utility workers," he explained, putting his gun in his waist and adjusting his ball cap so it hid more of his face.

"So, you think we gonna walk right in that bitch, huh? Okay, the Malibu left again, but there's still somebody in the house. I think we in the right place 'cause they didn't have the bag with 'em when they left," Max informed him, retrieving his gun and then dressing in the things Slugga had given him to wear.

The two hoodlums exited the van after moving it a little closer to their destination for an easy getaway. Moments later, Slugga was ringing the doorbell while holding a hammer and clipboard in his gloved hands. Max pretended to be looking for something in the work bag. In truth, he was only concealing the pistol grip 12-gauge pump that he was aiming at the door.

As soon as a short Latino opened the door to them, Slugga rushed the man, whacked him a few hard times with the hammer, and pushed him back inside the house. Max drew the gauge and rushed in right behind them, pointing the menacing-looking weapon at the heads of the other men in the house.

"Don't make this shit hard for yo'self! All we want is the money, and don't nobody gotta die in this bitch!" Slugga announced, with the bloody unconscious man lying at his feet.

He quickly snatched a mini assault rifle and a Glock 23 off the coffee table within reach of the other two men in the poorly furnished house.

"Okay, okay, just don't kill us. I'll give it to you," one of the men pleaded. "I'll give it to you. Just let my homey help his brother, and don't kill us," he bargained, holding his hands high so they would not think he was on anything bogus with them.

Slugga gave him his word, and the man took them to the money. Max forced the displeased occupants into a bedroom closet and told them to wait five minutes before they came out. He then went to help Slugga fill the bag with a variety of goods they wanted. To be on the safe side, Slugga blocked the closet door with a mattress before he and Max fled the place and the area. On the way out of the neighborhood, they passed the two guys in the Malibu on its return to the house.

"Where we heading? Yo' crib or mine?"

"Yours since it's closer, and I don't feel like explaining this money to the wife just yet. I'm gonna have to buy her something pretty to soften her up first," he laughed. "Ya did good in there. I didn't think ya had it in you like that."

"Aww, I thought ya knew I mean it when I say

I'm trained to go in whatever I'm on," Max told

him before he turned up the radio.

CHAPTER 2

The morning turned into mid-afternoon by the time Scrap sent a text to the girls telling them to come back to the club. Champagne decided to make him wait until she had her fingernails redone for work before she returned, but Playthang met up with him about fifteen minutes after receiving the text. She was hoping for some time alone with him, so she could thank him for standing up to Man-Man the night before when he overheard him and Badman talking trash about her.

"Be careful not to knock this over, 'cause

that's about fifty Gs ya workin' with right there. If ya do, then you bought it, and it will be on you to get it off," he cautioned her as he handed her a beer to sip on while he taught her how to cut and max that dope he needed to get ready for Man-Man.

"Oh no! No, I won't do that. But if you need me to help sell some of this, I'm down as long as you show me what to do," she said before she took a swallow of the beer. "Scrap, thanks for defending me last night. You're the first man to ever do that for me."

He took a step closer.

"Bitch, you're the one that started that shit!" Scrap said, grabbing her by the wrist and accidently breaking a thin gold bracelet she was wearing.

"What? No, no I didn't!"

Her wrist was hurting from the way he was squeezing it.

"I've never spoken to Man-Man before then."

"Yeah, bitch, ya started it! Look at you now, dressed like that just to tease a muthafucka," he stated as he pulled her away from the drugs, so she would not spill them on the floor. "You knew what you were coming here to do, so you didn't have to put on all that slutty shit."

"Scrap, let go of my arm! You're trippin'," Playthang whispered as she weakly tried to pull away.

The truth was that it was exciting to her. The way he was controlling her turned her on. But she did not want to pursue Scrap for a relationship until Champagne was out of the picture and she was complete as a woman. But something in the way he looked at her told her his antics were not as they seemed.

"Get away from me!"

He laughed as he stared into her eyes.

"Play, you goin' with that? You don't want me to get away from you. You want me to get in you, don't you?" he asked, letting up on his grip but not releasing her.

"It don't matter. Champ is my friend and you're her man. I can't do her like that."

"She's the one who put us together, so anything that goes on is on her," he said as he scooped up a bit of dope, sprinkled it on the back of his hand, and then snorted it. "You want some?" he asked while repeating the process and holding it out to her this time.

Playthang read into what he was implying and wanted to give in to him the way she dreamt of doing.

"But she's not here, and you saw how she was the last time. If she catches us, then what?" she asked, pulling his hand up to her face and snorting the powerful drug off it.

"I run this shit. Not her!" he spoke up as he pulled up her skirt around her waist to expose her blue lace panties.

He roughly squeezed her butt before slapping her on it and pulling her down onto his lap as he sat down in the chair they were standing in front of.

"Oooh, I like that rough shit!" Playthang almost purred. "Let's do a little more candy so I can get all the way in the mood."

She started sucking on his neck and working on his pants. Once she had them down and his hardness in her warm hand, she gently stroked it.

"Can I do some off of this?" she asked.

"Bitch, ya can do what you like as long as you put it in yo' mouth afterward," he answered, falling back in the seat so he could watch her blow him.

Playthang went and got some more of the dope and then sprinkled it onto Scrap's hard-on and snorted it off. She tossed her head back to get her hair out of her face, and then licked off the residue before taking him in her mouth.

* * *

Slugga took home his $210,000 from the robbery so his wife could bail out their son from jail while he paid the lawyer's fee to handle the case. While he was gone, Max took his cut of the money to the bank and locked it away in a safety deposit box. While standing in line, Max grabbed a brochure for a vacation spot in Mexico called Cabo Pulmo, since he had never been anywhere further than Chicago. He daydreamed of taking the trip when he got off probation in a few days.

After handling his business at the bank, Max headed downtown to a jeweler that he knew would accept the jewelry on trade. He entered the store behind a small group of teens that just seemed to be window shopping. The interior of the store displayed brightly lit showcases that were mostly filled with jewelry, but a few held purses, eyeglasses, and other fashion accessories. Two Asian saleswomen immediately steered the group of potential customers over to their sales area, and Max continued on toward the far end of the store.

The old man's face lit up when he noticed Max standing there. He yelled into the back and then finished tending to a couple of guys who were shopping for rings. The guy Max was there for came beaming through the door an instant later. Max exchanged greetings with him and then passed him the velvet Crown Royal bag containing the loot he wished to trade or sell. The jeweler took the bag in the back so he could inspect it before making an offer.

Before Max could decide on the pieces he wanted, and a nice ring that Slugga asked him to pick up for his wife, he received a text from Kake saying she needed to see him ASAP. He responded telling her to meet him at his house. He then took an in-store credit with the jeweler before leaving him with the goods and then leaving the store.

When Max pulled up in back of his house, he found Slugga and Kake sitting in his car smoking a blunt waiting on him.

"Kake, what's so important that ya needed to

see me ASAP?" he asked, noticing her cheerful mood.

"I'm out and I need some more," she proudly answered before handing him the money she made. "Can I get like two extra O's this time 'cause I had to turn down some money so I wouldn't run out on the rest of the people I had coming to cop, and I got a few waiting for me right now."

Greed was written all over Max's face. He had more money than he ever had in his life and the means to make more. Max had given Slugga the majority of the cash from the home invasion and kept $50,000 for himself and the drugs, since Slugga refused to sell anything other than weed and pills.

"Alright, I'ma give you a whole thang, but I got some shit to take care of, so ya gotta take it and go right away."

"That's cool! Just get up with me later. I ain't going into the club tonight, so we can get together and chill when ya got time. You owe me from last night anyway."

Max and Slugga went inside the house, leaving her sitting in the car. Moments later, Max returned carrying a black plastic shopping bag which he handed to Kake.

"I gave you three, so you won't have to miss no cash. Hey, when you get the money up, go grab two new phones. I don't want us talking on the same lines we do business on, okay?"

"Oh, I know better! I use my burner phone.

But I do got a few people who call my other phone, so I'll get on that right now, bae. I'll have 'em when ya come over, or do you need it right away?"

"No, that's cool. I'll get it then."

His phone rang.

"Let me go, and you be careful," he told her before he gave her a hug and let her kiss him on the cheek before she pulled off.

Max walked slowly back into his unit and responded to Tia's text message. She informed him that she would be returning from her grandmother's out-of-state funeral in two hours and needed to see him. It was then that Max realized that he genuinely cared for her. He sent her the web address listed on the brochure and asked her to think about going there with him. Tia said she would take it into consideration.

"Max, let's get this shit over with while I still got a good feeling about it," Slugga told Max when he walked in. "What you smiling about?'

"Nothing! I was just thinkin' about something, but whatever. Champ ain't called me yet, so fuck it! Let's just go handle this shit if we can. And if not, then she'll know we tried. Hell, I'll give the bitch ten Gs so she can get outta town like she wants to," Max told him.

He then walked to his bedroom to change back into the clothes he wore on the morning robbery. They then headed back to their spot across from Bonkerz.

CHAPTER 3

Champagne's phone battery died while she was getting a facial. It was not until she put it on the car charger that she received the flood of text messages and missed calls. Many were from Max trying to let her know he was ready to make his move. After picking up food from Dino's, she answered Max's text and also sent one to Scrap and Playthang to let them know she was on her way and that she would pick up corned beef sandwiches for them.

Upon turning into the lot, Champagne did not notice the two thugs watching her while parked across from Bonkerz. She parked and then got out of her car while cautiously holding the bag of hot food so it would not mess up her outfit or freshly done fingernails. She then made her way inside the club's side entrance. When she entered the office, she found them in another knotty predicament.

"What the fuck is y'all doing!"

Even though it was part of her plan, this was still a shock, and even more so when she noticed Scrap was snorting lines off of Playthang's body. The two of them jumped at the sound of her voice.

"Champ, where the fuck ya been?" he asked, ignoring her question and not even making an effort to clean the powder from his nose.

"We're just having some fun. Come play with us," her friend explained, sliding her hand inside of Scrap's boxers like it was okay to do in front of her.

"Bitch, fuck you!"

Champagne noticed Playthang's bloodshot eyes and knew she was just as high as he was. This made her worry if she had told Scrap what they were planning in her wasted state of mind.

"Bitch, get the fuck up! I ain't doing this shit with y'all. You muthafuckas are too high," she said as she shook her head. "I'm so done with you, nigga!"

She dropped the bag and made a tight fist like she was going to swing at Scrap.

"Ohhhhh, you mad at me again?" Playthang

asked in a child-like tone and then giggled.

"What's this?" he asked, ignoring her small fist and picking up the bag off the floor as he stood up off his knees.

"I gotta use the bathroom. Save me some of that in that bag," Playthang said while getting up off the floor and spilling the remaining drug on her belly onto the floor.

She tried to kiss Champagne on her way out of the room but got pushed away instead.

"Don't be like that. I'ma just doing what I gotta do," she said with a smile and walked out.

"Scrap, how could you do me like this again? I'm so done with you. I can't stand yo' punk ass!" she snapped, hoping that she had read her friend right and it wasn't just the drugs talking.

"Bitch, go on with the punk shit! Don't make me!"

Before he could finish his statement, Playthang was shoved through the door by two armed masked men.

"Don't fuckin' move, and shit don't gotta get messy," one of the men shouted while holding his gun on Playthang. "We just wanna rob ya, not boost the body count on the news."

The other man quickly grabbed Champagne by the neck and then spun her around and pointed his gun at Scrap.

"Be cool, Champ; it's me," he whispered into her ear.

"You niggas must be lost," Scrap said as he took a bite of the sandwich he was holding like he did not have a care in the world. "Just let my bitches go, turn around, and get the fuck outta here, and it won't be nothing," he told them unfazed.

Slugga kicked Playthang to the floor and then rushed across the room and smacked Scrap with the gun, knocking him off his feet.

"Bitch, ya ain't running shit, so stay the fuck down!"

Max made the girls load up the bags. Champagne worked on the open safe while Max made Playthang load up the unopened blocks of dope into a Batman knapsack.

Playthang was unaware of her friend's involvement in the robbery, so she made up her mind to try to save the day. She snatched up the gun that was hidden from the robbers behind the stacks of dope.

"Drop your guns and get out!" Playthang yelled as she quickly spun around and pointed the gun at Max.

Slugga had moved closer to her when her back was turned. He kicked her in the midsection and grabbed her hand that was holding the gun. The surprise from his attack caused her to pull the trigger, sending hot lead flying past Max and into the computer on the desk. Slugga hit her hard in the head, which made Playthang's grip loosen on the gun, which he quickly snatched from her hand. Slugga gave her another hard knee in her chest, which knocked the wind out of her. When Playthang dropped to the floor, he kicked her the rest of the way down.

"Stay the fuck down, bitch, before I kill you!" Slugga said, now with his gun to her head. "Bro, you good?" he asked Max.

"Yeah, I'm good. Let's hurry up, 'cause somebody might've heard that shot," he answered.

He turned to Champagne and ordered her to finish loading up her bag while he stuffed as many of the bricks inside the knapsack as he could and then tossed it over his shoulder.

Champagne emptied the safe and handed the duffel bag to Slugga. Max grabbed her and used her as a shield as they made their way out of the office. At the door, Max turned out the lights and lightly pushed Champagne to the floor before making his escape.

Scrap rushed over to her when she came violently stumbling off the stairs.

"Champ, you alright?" he asked, turning on the lights and helping her to her feet.

"Yeah, I'm okay, I'm okay. Play, is you okay?" she asked, rushing over to her friend and wishing she did not have to get hurt for them to get the money.

It was then that Champagne decided to take Play with her when she skipped town.

"I thought he was going to kill me," she said with tears running down her face.

"Come on, let's get outta here!" she said, helping her to her feet.

"What? Where you going?" Scrap asked, putting the code into the other safe.

"I don't know! Home! I just wanna get the fuck away from here. Play, come on," Champagne said, kneeling to collect the spilled contents of her purse off the floor not far from where Playthang was sitting.

"Yeah, I just need to put some ice on my cheek. I can feel it swelling," she groaned as she picked herself up off the floor and limped over to the refrigerator to get what she needed. "Champagne, do you got something for pain in your purse?" Playthang asked, holding a cold bottled water against her face before taking a drink of it.

"No, but we can stop and get something on

the way to my house. I don't wanna be here when them fools get here," she answered while shaking her head.

She stood up and looked at the mess that Max and his partner had made during the robbery.

"Champ, I can't call them niggers. I gotta fix this shit myself. I need to think," Scrap told her, raking up a long line of the powerful narcotic that was smeared across the tabletop. He snorted half of it and then said, "No, I can't call them. I need y'all to help me get these orders together. I gotta try to make that money back before tonight."

He snorted the rest of the line and started to scrape up another one.

"No, Scrap, put that shit down. What the fuck is happening then? What's going on tonight, Scrap?" Champagne demanded, standing over him with her hand on her hip while clutching her keys in the other.

"Murdah's comin' to pick it up, that's what," he informed her as he tossed his head back to catch the drain of the drug. "The good thing is they didn't get in the other safes, so I'm about halfway there. But I gotta do this shit without Bad finding out what happened first. I know he's still in his chest about the other night," Scrap explained while lookin' from one face to the other. "I need y'all to stay here to be sure that don't happen. I don't need ya to slip up and say shit to anyone and to help me with this."

"Not gonna happen. Ya know I ain't gonna say shit to nobody. I can't do this shit with you, Scrap. Look at you right now. You're a fuckin' mess! I'm going home. Play, let's go."

"Champ, I'ma stay here and help him with this. He can't do it all by himself," she answered as she started fixing up a line for herself. "I'll call you later, okay?" Playthang promised, giving Champagne a quick wink and smile before dropping her face into the pile.

Champagne shook her head and stomped out of the office. Scrap was right on her heels telling her to go straight home and remain there until he told her differently. She wanted to tell him to go to hell, but she did not want him to stop her from leaving. As soon as she was away from the club, she pulled out her phone and texted Max to tell him that she was on her way home. She did a little happy dance when she came to a stop sign. Champagne hated that they did not get to clean out Scrap, but from what she had seen, they still had taken a lot of cash from him. She wondered if there was a way to get the rest of it or all of what Max had, since he was the keeping all of the drugs they took. Champagne was plotting her next move when Max responded telling her to stay with Scrap until she heard from him, because he did not want him to suspect she had anything to do with the robbery.

Champagne did not want to go back, but she knew Max was right, so she decided to drive around to calm her nerves before returning.

* * *

After returning to Max's place, they noticed an unfamiliar gray Subaru parked behind the house.

"Hey, do you know whose car that belongs to?" Slugga asked, adjusting himself in his seat.

"Nope, I was just about to ask you the same shit," Max answered as he slowed his approach and retrieved his gun from between the seat just in case he needed it. "Let's be ready for whatever. Ya know them niggas better than I do."

Slugga lowered his window and gripped his gun as he strained to see who was inside the vehicle. He was the first to see the female sitting on Max's steps.

"It's some chick sitting on yo' porch, bro," he informed his partner as he continued to search the area for an ambush just to be safe.

Tia's ringtone began playing on Max's phone. He picked it up knowing it was a text.

"Man, that might be Tia. She's texting me right now and askin' me where I'm at," he said as he pulled in next to the car. "Yeah, that's her ass. She must've wanted to surprise me 'cause she said she wasn't gonna be back for a couple of hours," he confirmed, smiling once he was able to see her.

"Well, yo' in-love ass needs to get rid of her right quick, 'cause she's still them people and I'm not trying to get caught up on no humbug shit!"

"Alright, just take this shit into the crib while I holla at her," Max told him as he handed him the keys and his gun.

"Bro, ya better hold on to that 'cause we still ain't heard from ol' girl yet, and it's better to be safe than dead," Slugga informed him as he pushed the gun back to him and then grabbed the bags and got out.

He walked with his head down and his hood up so Tia would not get a good look at his face as he went by.

"Hey, you! I thought ya was still in the air. What happened?" Max asked her as she stood up and greeted him with a kiss and hug.

He noticed she was dressed down in a pair of white K Swiss with form-fitting jeans and a white cotton smiley-face shirt.

"I wanted to surprise you and maybe catch you doing some of your sexy thug shit," Tia answered, showing her pretty smile.

"You a mess." He laughed as he shook his head. "But, ma, I'm in the middle of somethin' that I don't want you around. As soon as I'm done, I'll be over so I can show ya how much I've missed you."

"So that's why your friend hid his face from me just now?"

She gave him a lustful kiss before returning to her rental car and driving away.

Max walked into his unit, where Slugga was on the phone with his wife. That's when he received the text they were waiting for from

Champagne, but it was not what he wanted to hear. Max texted her back and told her to stay with Scrap so he would not get suspicious. He promised he would call her when he was ready for her. He then emptied the bags onto the table so he and Slugga could divide up the money among the three of them. Max planned on keeping the drugs, so his cut would be a lot smaller than theirs, but his profit would be greater in the end.

"Bruh, let's do this later. I gotta run to the crib. Sara's trippin' on me. She wants me to go with her to pick up my son from the house. I hate going to that muthafucka's place, but if I don't go, I won't hear the last of it."

"Go handle yo' business. I'ma be over Tia's

'til ya ready. I already told Champ to stay with ol' boy for a minute, so she could keep us posted on what he on and shit."

"Say no mo'! I'ma hit you as soon as I make it back," Slugga said, helping him stuff the loot back into the bags. "Don't forget to pick up that ring for me. I'ma need it when I tell her about this shit. So, make sure it's nice and blingy. If you have to use some of yo' cut of that shit, just take it outta this here."

"I got ya, my nigga. Don't worry about that. If I gotta use all that shit to get her something phat, it's all good."

When they were done filling the bags, Max removed the cover from the heater vent in the bathroom floor and stuffed the bags inside until they returned. Trust was not an issue between the two of them, but they were dealing with a third party and did not trust her.

CHAPTER 4

Tia received Max's text just as she finished unpacking her bags from the trip and the few things she picked up to make dinner when he came by. She responded and let him know that she was about to take a much-needed bath and that the door was unlocked for him. The lust-filled thoughts running through her mind as she undressed made her nervously excited and made it hard to keep her hands off herself. Tia wanted and needed Max inside of her. She changed her mind once she got into the bathroom, and she decided to take a shower and save the bath for after her wild roll between the sheets.

Max let himself in as planned. He was feeling a little frisky, so he decided to have some fun with Tia. As quietly as he could, he slipped back outside, ran back to his truck for his black bandana and gloves, and then eased back inside the house, leaving the door unlocked so she would not know he was hiding behind the sofa. His wait was not long. Tia emerged from the bathroom glowing with beauty. She was dressed in only a pink-and-powder-blue towel, which teased him with her long legs.

Tia scanned the room as she crossed it to check the door. When she found it unlocked, her smile faded some but returned when she saw his footprints on the carpet. She knew he was inside hiding somewhere. The thought of Max jumping out on her added fuel to the excitement she was already feeling. Wondering if he was someplace that he could see her, Tia let the towel drop to the floor on her way back to her bedroom. She also added an extra twist in her hips for his enjoyment. She pushed the door closed and pressed play on the radio. She sat on the bed and slowly moisturized her body, pretending not to notice the sound the door made when Max slipped into the room behind her as she sung offkey and swayed to Alisha Keys's soulful voice.

"Don't scream!" Max ordered her, covering her mouth with his gloved hand.

Tia froze, trying her best to play the part of a helpless woman while fighting the heat building between her thighs. She dropped the bottle of shea butter she was using on her legs and covered her breasts with her hands.

"Now when I uncover yo' sexy-ass lips, do you promise not to scream and do as ya told?" he asked, holding her tight to his body.

Feeling Max so close and the way he was dominating her made her hotter for him. She nodded and looked him right in his eyes through the mirror in front of which they were now standing.

"Please don't hurt me. I'm—!"

Max clamped his hand back over her mouth.

"I didn't tell you to say shit. Now, bitch, I gotta teach ya how to follow directions."

He dragged his hands slowly down her body.

The warm leather felt good on her skin. Suddenly he scooped her off her feet and tossed her onto the bed. As Tia fell, she snatched the bandana off of his face and then quickly rolled away from him, snatching a hairbrush off the nightstand.

"Stop or I'll shoot!" she yelled, pointing the pretend gun at him. "You thought you had an easy one, didn't you? Nigga, I seen yo' footprints in the carpet and heard the room door when you came in," she explained, standing up on her knees on the bed.

"Wow. Please don't kill me, lady. I just couldn't help myself when I seen yo' sexy ass comin' in here," Max played along, holding his hands high in the air. "Hands up, don't shoot!"

"Yeah, is this what you want?" She cupped one of her breasts and then brought it up to her mouth, where she flicked her tongue across her nipple. Max nodded.

"Show me you want me. Come get me."

Max started removing his clothes while she repositioned herself on the bed with her long legs spread wide to invite him in. He grabbed her by the ankles and pulled her to him as he took his place between them.

"You better hurry, because my man's on his way home," she told him, still playing the role.

"Fuck him! I'll deal with him when he gets here. But, baby, I ain't rushing this here. You made me wait way too long," he said before he silenced her by kissing her hard on the mouth while slowly pressing his hardness into her wetness.

* * *

Slugga and his wife were sitting outside of the house of corrections waiting for their son to be released, when sirens and flashing lights from ambulances and other emergency vehicles began flooding the parking lot.

"I wonder what's going on?"

"Somebody got fucked up! That's what happened!"

"I hope this shit don't hold up Terry's release. I'm going to go in there and find out," Sara said while closing the sales paper she was reading.

Suddenly a K-9 squad car pulled into the slot next to them, and the dogs went wild barking at them and jumping on the side of the car.

"Fuck!" Slugga dropped his head in his hands.

"What's wrong?"

"That mutt must smell the lil' weed I got on me. I brought it for Terry to celebrate his release with his girl, so he wouldn't be in the streets too quick."

As soon as Slugga finished his statement, the cop ordered them to unlock the doors and place their hands where he could see them.

"What's goin' on?" Slugga asked as he did what the officer said and then played dumb.

"My partner and I have reason to believe that you have drugs in there with you. So would you please step out of the car and allow us to have a look."

"No! You need a warrant. You just can't be fuckin' with us," Sara said, cutting him off.

"Chill! Let's not make this hard for us," Slugga told her. "My wife and I are just here to pick up my son. I smoke a little and forgot that I got a sack on me. That's it, it's nothing big."

"If that's all it is, you shouldn't have an issue with me searching your car!" the cop said with his hand on his gun.

"No, ya good, so could you put the dog up, please?"

The officer ordered the dog to relax, and then Slugga and Sara got out of the car. Slugga was cuffed right away and patted down. Just like Slugga said, the officer found two grams of weed on him. Other officers came rushing across the parking lot.

"I'm sorry to have to do this to you, sir, but I'm going to have to take you in because you're on county property. If we were anyplace else, I would've just made you dump it out," the officer said before the first officer made it over to them.

Slugga told Sara to get their son and go home until he called her, since the cop had assured him that he would not charge him with a felony and that she could go inside.

Slugga passed his son on the way to be placed in a holding cell until he could be processed.

"Your mom is outside waiting for you. Make sure she goes home until I call. This ain't shit!" Slugga yelled to his son as they passed.

CHAPTER 5

Champagne returned to Bonkerz with coffee. She felt it would be best to sober up Playthang so she did not slip up and say anything that Champagne did not want Scrap to know. Scrap's face lit up when she walked into the office.

"Don't get happy. I'm still mad at you," Champagne said, stopping him in his tracks. "I'm only here to make sure my friend is okay and get her away from yo' manipulative ass."

Scrap took one of the large coffees from the tray she was holding and sipped it.

"I know the truth. Yo' fine ass didn't just come back for that. Ya know you can't live without daddy," he told her, sliding his free hand around her waist and giving her butt a squeeze as he kissed her on the forehead.

Champagne pushed past him with her shoulder.

"Boy, please!" she called out as she made her way over to Playthang and immediately noticed that her face was more bruised than it was before she left. "Oh my God! Play, how come you don't got ice on yo' face?"

"Champ, Champ, I'm okay. He didn't mean to do it. Scrap was just mad that all this happen-ed," Playthang answered, clearly wasted from all the drugs she had been doing with Scrap.

"What are you saying? Did Scrap do this to you?" Champagne demanded, kneeling down in front of her friend with the tray.

"Champ, it's okay," Playthang tried to assure her as she took a coffee for herself. "You read my mind. This is just what I needed."

Champagne was so hurt seeing her friend like this because of her. All she could do was wait for Max to call.

"We leaving this asshole as soon as I get the okay I'm waiting on," she told Playthang with a hug as she whispered her apologies. "I really didn't mean for none of this to happen to you, but I'll make it up to you and give ya the money ya need and take you with me."

"Why in the fuck did you do this to her?"

Champagne yelled when she turned toward Scrap.

"Bitch, who in the fuck do ya think you're talkin' to? The bitch is lucky I ain't still beating her ass for not fighting back. We could've handled them niggas."

"Fuck you! Fuck this! Play, get up and let's go!"

When Champagne turned back to face Scrap, he punched her in the side of her head and pulled his gun on her.

"Bitch, go sit yo' dumb ass down. As a matter of fact, I think she used yo' fool ass to get close to me. Yeah, I think her ass had somethin' to do with this shit."

With that said, he started repeatedly

punching Playthang and demanding for her to tell him something she really did not know. She denied having anything to do with the robbery. When she called someone and walked out of the office to use the restroom, he took things further in his rage by pistol whipping her. Before long, Playthang fell unconscious at his feet. Champagne was frozen by fear, since she had never seen him act this way. As much as she wanted to stop him from beating her friend, she was afraid that he would start beating on her, so she kept her mouth shut.

"Bitch, get over here and help me with this punk!"

"No, no! I can't!"

"Bitch, don't tell me what ya ain't gonna do,"

he told her, forcing her to help him drag her into the punishment room and tie up Playthang.

When she was done, he made her go back into the office and have a seat.

Champagne saw that Scrap was really wilding out at this point, and all she could do was pray that he did not turn on her in his drugged-up, psychotic state of mind.

"Calm down, baby. Scrap, please just calm down!" she begged as she took hold of his back pants pocket and stopped him as he paced the room. "Talk to me. Why do you think Play had something to do with what happened?" she pleaded, sliding her hand up and down his legs. "Come sit down with me."

She was doing her best to seduce him into

letting his guard down and not going back inside with her friend.

"Don't worry about that. Just suck a nigga's dick or something so I can think," he told her, running his bloody hand down the back of her head and gently tugging her hair.

Champagne did not want to be touched by him, but if that was what it was going to take to keep him from killing Playthang, she would do whatever he wanted.

"Only if you tell me why ya think she had somethin' to do with that shit," she tried to bargain with him as she slowly worked on his belt while rubbing the length of his hard-on through his pants.

"Just think about it. The bitch has been on

this shit from the start. She and Man-Man are in this shit together. I know he got shit to do with this 'cause he called and changed up his order right after it happened. He knew I don't got enough to cover the order no more."

"I still don't see how she has anything to do with it. They beat her up when she tried to help, remember?" Champagne reminded him, now with his pants down to his knees and stroking his hardness with her soft, warm hand.

"Play let them niggas in here when she acted like she was going to the bathroom. The bitch tried to make it seem like ya must've forgot to lock the door when ya left earlier. But I know better," he told her before he placed the gun down next to her as his mood slowly changed from anger to lust. "Murdah's gonna be here to pick up the money and some later. He's coming himself because some shit happened earlier with the connect. I'm not dumb. Shit don't just happen like that!"

"Babe, just tell Badman that and let him deal with it."

"Fuck that!" Scrap pulled away from her. "I ain't gonna let them make me seem weak," he yelled as he pulled up his pants. "I'ma wake that punk up and make her tell me everything."

Scrap snatched up the gun and rushed out of the office. Champagne did not try to stop him, because she did not want him to turn on her.

She could hear Playthang's cries from the beating that Scrap was putting on her.

Champagne could almost feel the hard blows herself because of the guilt she was feeling for putting her friend up to this. Champagne got up and got her phone from her bag, and sent Max a text for help. She did not know who else to call.

* * *

Max was lying in bed breathless and sweaty, enjoying the after-effects of their powerful release. He had gotten so caught up in the rape robbery fantasy that he pushed the earlier activities of his day out of his mind. He could not believe the effect that Tia had on him, nor could he understand where the feelings were coming from. Tia had just dipped her head under the sheet to try to jumpstart round two, when Champagne's ringtone snapped Max back to reality.

"Damn, ma, yo' ass made me lose track of what I got going on."

"No, Max, don't blame me. Whatever you forgot is on you. You're the one that started this. Here, answer yo' phone. I gotta pee anyway," she told him after handing him his phone and leaving the room.

"Bring me somethin' back to drink!" he yelled behind her as he opened Champagne's text, thinking she was just wondering if he had skipped town on her with her cut:

"I need to get outta here. 911."

"Why, is he on to you?"

"No. He's gone crazy. He thinks my friend set him up. We gotta get outta here."

"That's some good shit, so just chill. I'ma hit ya in a sec."

"No! I'm scared he's gonna kill her. He's high and crazy."

"Can you go somewhere and call me?"

Champagne called him right away.

"Max, what's wrong? You look upset," Tia asked, returning with two cold Rockstar drinks.

"Ummm, shit! Let me deal with this here right quick, and then I'll holla at you about it," he told her before he walked into the bathroom, closed the door behind him, and answered the call. "Champ, where the nigga at now? Is y'all still at the spot?"

"Yeah, we still here. Scrap's crazy ass is beating on her like she's a dog. He's gonna kill her, I can't leave her here," she answered with real fear in her voice.

"Okay, okay. Do ya know who he thinks helped her? Did he say anything?"

"He thinks it's Man-Man and 'em. Play don't know shit about you. I promise she don't."

"Okay, I believe you," Max said, hearing Scrap come into the background fussing just before the line went dead.

Max knew Champagne had hung up on him so she would not get caught talking to him; therefore, he did not call back. Instead, he sent Slugga a 911 text as he rushed to get dressed.

"Whoa, where you rushing off to? What's going on? Should I be getting dressed?" Tia asked with concern based on his sudden change in mood and eagerness to leave.

"Nope! Look, I can't tell ya what's going on right now 'cause I gotta go, but I promise I will tell you everything as soon as I'm done. All I can say right now is a friend of mine is in trouble, and I gotta go help her."

"Her? Who? Okay, never mind. Just be careful and try not to have any police contact. Max, you're too close to mess it all up now."

This was Tia's way of reminding him that she was still his parole officer. After he got dressed, he kissed her and rushed out the house to his truck. As he drove, he repeatedly tried calling Slugga, until he finally received a text from Sara informing him that her husband was in jail and that she was waiting on Slugga to call so she could bail him out.

When Max asked Sara what had happened, all she told him was that it was nothing major. Max had to handle things on his own. He could not believe how things flipped from good to bad. Max took a second to think, and prayed that things did not get worse. But just in case, he headed home to arm himself and get out of his truck. He still had not come up with a plan. All he knew was that leaving Champagne hanging was not an option, unless he wanted her to tell Scrap about him once her friend told him that Champagne had paid her to set him up.

* * *

Champagne hid her phone behind her back as she turned to face her tormentor who was ranting about Playthang. Champagne needed to take Scrap's mind off of her friend. She knew he could not stand to see her cry, so she began the waterworks. The sight of Playthang's blood on his hands made it easier for her to burst into tears.

"Baby, she didn't have nothing to do with this shit. I promise you she didn't. Please stop and let me take her to the hospital. I'll tell them she got jumped. They'll believe us because she's trans. Please?" Champagne told him as she slipped her phone into her pocket and walked closer to him.

"No! The punk was about to tell me, but the bitch passed out before she could say anything," Scrap said before he stopped pacing. "I gotta get everything together so I can get this money up. Bad's gonna be here in a minute, and I'ma need the cash from the house. It should put me right where I need to be."

"What you gonna do? It's almost time to open the club, and you're not thinkin' right."

"Bitch, I got this!" he snapped. "I ain't opening it tonight. I already sent a text to everybody tellin' 'em we ain't.'"

"What are you gonna tell Badman?"

"If I ain't got what I need to know outta Play, then I'ma make Man-Man tell on himself in front of him. His bitch ass don't know what I know and don't know, but when he sees the beating I put down, he's gonna think I was told something."

This was not what Champagne was asking

him, but it gave her an idea.

"This is so fuckin' crazy. I can't stay here and watch you beat my friend to death for something she didn't do. I gotta get outta here 'cause I don't want nothing to do with this shit. Let me go get the money while you get that together for 'em."

"No, I'm not letting you leave, because you won't come back," he told her with the crazy look returning in his eyes.

"Scrap, ya trippin'! Move! I'm finna go check on Play."

Scrap drew his gun from his back pocket.

"Bitch, I'm tryin' to be nice, but you ain't letting me!" he yelled as he made a fist. "Hoe, if ya ain't with me, then you must be against me, too."

"Baby, you too high right now. I didn't say that. That shit is making you act crazy," she said, softening her voice while trying not to set him all the way off again.

"Maybe, maybe not! It's a good guess 'cause you the one who brought her here. I bet y'all tried to get me caught up in all that freaky shit so I'll be off my square. Yeah, I know, bitch. I know."

"Baby, ya don't really believe that shit, do you? I love you. I just wanna get my friend some help and for you to calm down. That's all. Please, put the gun down," she begged him, letting her tears fall down freely from her face and hoping he would feel sorry for her and do as she asked.

"Sit the fuck down!" he yelled as he shoved her into the chair next to which she was standing. "Ya can stop that! Naw, that crying shit ain't gonna help you. Yeah, all you muthafuckas in this shit together," Scrap screamed as he got up into her face. "How long you been fuckin' him?"

"What? Who you talking about?"

"Murdah. I see the way y'all be acting when ya get together. I bet yo' ass wants this shit to go bad for me so y'all can get together. Don't you?"

Before she could answer, he started raining hard slaps across her head and face like a madman. Thinking he might start hitting her with the gun, Champagne tried to fight back. She brought her knees up to her chest and then kicked out with both legs as hard as she could. The force sent Scrap flying backward and Champagne crashing to the floor in the chair. She hit her head hard, which dazed her a bit. By the time the stars cleared, Scrap was back on his feet with his gun aimed at her face.

"Stupid bitch!"

"Scrap, no, don't!" she screamed, throwing her hands up to shield her face, like they could stop a bullet.

Something about it worked, because his expression changed and he lowered the gun.

"Oooh shit, I'm sorry," he said as he looked at the gun in his hand and then back at her. "Champ, baby. If I'm trippin', show me I'm wrong. Prove to me I am. Help me," he told her, looking sad and remorseful.

"Okay, okay, anything, baby. Anything you want. Just don't hit me no more," she pleaded, just as the doorbell rang.

"Straighten yo'self up. Come on," he ordered her as he checked the surveillance monitor and hid his gun in his waist behind his back and covered it with his shirt.

Scrap helped Champagne up onto her feet. She went along with him. She knew that if she did not, he would kill her and her friend before Max got there or before she could think of a way to save the two of them on her own.

* * *

Back in a dark corner of the Bonkerz parking

lot, Max sat slumped down in his rental as he tried to figure out his next move. Badman arrived and parked next to the front entrance of the club. Max slouched down even more as he tried his best not to be seen while still keeping the car full of goons in his sight. While he was checking his phone to see if he had missed any calls from Slugga or Champagne, the three men got out of the Audi and waited to be let inside.

Max knew that even with the element of surprise, he would not be able to get Champagne and her friend out of there on his own, but he had to try.

CHAPTER 6

Badman was the first through the door, followed by Man-Man and Big Tone. The narcissistic smirk on Man-Man's face annoyed Scrap even more, but he held it together and greeted them as if it was just another pickup.

"What up, fam? Why you ain't opening this joint up tonight?" Big Tone asked, looking around the empty club.

"There's just too much going on right now, plus my nigga told me the inspector's doing popups and might be hitting here in the morning. So I'ma take tonight to make sure everything's in order in this bitch so we won't have no issues," Scrap explained as he followed them over to the bar where Champagne was sitting and fondling her hair, trying to put it back in place from her tussle with Scrap.

"Naw, nigga. I see what you on in this bitch for real," Badman joked while smiling at Champagne. "What's good, Champ? Is this a private show for us, or did ya finally let this nigga lock that ass down? Let me know if he ain't hittin' that right, ma. Ya know a nigga like me can upgrade yo' whole world."

"Bad, go on with that shit," Scrap told him, cutting off the playful flirting. "Champ, get up and make us drinks. Pour up some shots and Coronas while I holla at fam," Scrap ordered her.

He then walked Badman away from the others, so he could talk to him in private to see how much he knew about the robbery before he called Man-Man out on it.

Badman took his time openly watching Champagne's wide hips and butt slide off the barstool until she disappeared behind the counter. Scrap's blood was already hot from all that had gone on already, and with his mind racing, this made all the usual stares and comments his girl received every day inflame him even more.

"Fam, what's the deal? Why y'all change up the order and shit?" Scrap asked, watching Badman watch Champagne tend to the guys at the bar.

"I told you the plug got hit today and I'm trippin'. Murdah thinks if he hits them with enough bread, they won't stop fuckin' with us, But to be on the safe side, I got another connect lined up that I'ma hit up to see what it can do. Ya should go in with me so we can lock shit down for real. Feel me?"

"Is folks good with that shit?"

"Man-Man tried to holla at him about it, but he's on one trying to help find out who's behind the robberies, so this shit's on us. If we lock it down, he ain't gonna trip. It's good. Is ya in or what?"

"Mmm, fam, I don't trust the shit that nigga Man-Man says."

"Whoa, my nigga! If ya got something to say about folks, say it to his face. But I'ma need you niggas to stop acting like bitches over that dumb shit so we can get this plug right. So, let's go get this shit cleared up."

With that said, Badman started walking back over by the others without waiting for Scrap's response.

At the bar, Champagne noticed them walking back and Scrap watching her every move. She was trying to think of a way to warn Man-Man about what Scrap was thinkin', so they could help Playthang and save them from him. Just as she was about to make her move, her phone began vibrating in her pocket. There were two short bursts at a time, which let her know it was a text. Without thinking, she pulled her phone out to check the message and prayed it was from Max.

"What you doing? No phones. Turn it off now!" Scrap snapped at her.

She quickly read, responded to, and deleted the text by the time he made it over to her. She feared that he might take away her phone. When he did not ask for the phone, she put it back in her pocket and grabbed two more shot glasses on the bar and handed a beer to Scrap. The look in his eyes made her take her drink and sit at the far end of the bar away from them. She also wanted to be out of view so she could use her phone. Champagne was able to keep her cool a bit better knowing that Max was outside somewhere planning to come save her. She imagined him out there with some of his goons all armed and ready to bust in to get her out of the mess she had started.

"Say, fam," Badman said, getting Man-Man's attention as he took a seat on the bar stool between him and Scrap. "You and folks gotta get straight and get off that bullshit. This nigga is still feelin' some type of way, so y'all need to get it in or drop it. We don't do this shit. Real niggas don't beef over bitches and petty shit."

"I'm good, it's MOB with me all day and every day; but if a nigga still in his chest about the shimmy, we can do it," he responded, flashing his gold-toothed smile that quickly faded into a menacing frown.

Before things could go further, Badman received a text from Murdah.

"Yeah, fuck that shit! It's dead for now. Folks on his way back, so let's handle our business and get this paper together. Y'all fools can do what y'all want when we done with this shit," he told them while answering the text. "Scrap, go run and grab that work I need and all that bread, so we can bust that move before he gets here."

Scrap gulped down his drink and then looked dead at Champagne and waved his empty glass for her to come refill it.

"Did he say how long before he gets here?" he asked, not taking his eyes off of Champagne until she got the bottle to refill all of their glasses.

He could see fear in her eyes, which made

him believe they were all playing him.

"Nope, but he's coming from Minnesota, so we got a good four hours," Badman answered while responding to another text. "Fam, how much bread can ya pull together right now for this shit?"

"I don't know. I still gotta get my count together from that bullshit down at the crib the other day. How much do we need?"

"Shit, about three hundred Gs if we really wanna show them we ain't playin' in these streets. But I don't have a number. I didn't give 'em one yet 'cause I wanted to holla at you first."

"So that's like $1.6 million altogether," Man-Man said, followed by a whistle. "That's that paper right there. But it shouldn't be shit for ol'

Scrappy Doo here to pull outta his ass. Fam should just put the whole three hundred up and take it off the top so we can get this shit movin'!"

This was all it took for Scrap to lose it again.

"Oh, you' funny, nigga. Huh, nigga, ya think I'm stupid? Am I a stupid nigga to you?"

"Scrap?"

"Shut the fuck up, bitch, before I get on yo' ass again. Right now, this is between me and them, unless ya choosing? Is ya choosing, Champ?" he snapped at her, cutting her off before she got out what she wanted to say.

"What the fuck just happened?" Big Tone demanded, with a cloud of weed smoke surrounding his head from the blunt he was smoking.

"Fam, didn't I just say we don't got time for this petty shit," Badman said, putting his beer down and anticipating having to break up a fight.

"Naw, fall back, fam. This ain't that. These niggas know what I'm talking about. Y'all wanna tell him yo'self, or should I tell him?" Scrap said while repositioning himself so that he had all of them in his sights just in case one of them decided to run up on him.

Champagne was frozen by her fear, and all she could do was watch as Big Tone slammed his beer down on the bar and jumped off his seat to intervene and clear up any misunderstanding concerning himself. She saw Scrap whip out his gun from behind his back before anyone else did.

"Don't make another muthafuckin' move, Tone!" Scrap barked at him while waving the gun from the big man's face and back to Man-Man.

"What the hell you on, Scrap? Put that burner down!" Badman ordered, taking a step closer to him.

"Folks, it was these bitch-ass niggas that robbed me. They tryin' to play us. Champ knows," he announced as he looked her way. "Bae, tell him what happened today."

"Robbed you? Nigga, I ain't gotta rob yo' soft ass. I'll take what I want, bitch!"

Scrap turned the gun on Man-Man and shot him in the gut. Nobody could believe what just had happened. Badman moved to take the gun from him, startling Scrap and causing him to squeeze the trigger twice more. Badman was hit with slugs at close range that spun him around before he hit the floor hard, smashing his head on a bar stool.

Champagne dropped to the floor behind the bar counter for cover fearing for her life. Big Tone dove behind the corner of the bar while simultaneously drawing his own gun. But before he could take aim, Scrap sent four shots his way, hitting him in the throat and face and instantly killing his big friend.

"Help me!" Man-Man begged in a childlike voice, holding the gushing wound in his stomach.

"Yeah, fuck you!" Scrap yelled before he

then shot him three more times in the chest and head. "You bitches think y'all can fuck me over! Ya think I got bitch in my blood! Y'all must've forgot how I get down!" he yelled at the bodies while crazily pacing in circles and still squeezing the trigger of the now-empty gun at his side.

Champagne texted Max from her hiding place and let him know to get her now.

CHAPTER 7

Playthang slowly regained consciousness as the pain from the beating Scrap put on her kicked in, and remembered that her life was in danger. She thrashed around wildly as she struggled to break free of the black zip ties holding her hands and feet together. Moments after fully regaining consciousness, several gunshots broke the silence to let her know that she was not alone. Playthang knew there was no time for crying. She needed to get free if she wanted to live. She stopped fighting with the ties and looked around the room for something to use. That was when a soda can caught her attention across the room.

"Thank you, Lord!" she said aloud, letting the last of her fears be replaced with hope as she inched her way across the floor.

Playthang painfully rolled over potentially broken ribs until she was close enough to the can. Once it was in her hands, she twisted it back and forth until it ripped apart, cutting her palm in the process. Playthang did not let that stop her. She sawed through the tie with the sharp, jagged can until she was able break her hands free. She then went to work on her feet. Once she was free, Playthang crawled to the door and took a quick moment to listen to the

ASSA RAYMOND BAKER

next room before climbing to her feet. She carefully opened the door and crept out.

* * *

Crouched down beside the dumpster in the dark parking lot was as far as Max made it when gunfire started inside Bonkerz. He froze at the sound and the buzzing of his phone in his pocket. He read the text from Champagne rushing him to do something. Max's plan did not involve whatever was going on in there. He took a moment to think. That was when a female burst out of the side door that he used to commit the robbery. Whoever it was quickly lumped away into the darkness carrying something big. He knew from the height that it was not

Champagne, but his luck was the open door. It was just what he needed to get inside unnoticed and then to get her out.

Just as he readied himself to move, an unmarked squad car came creeping into the parking lot, forcing him to fall back and watch how things played out.

Max eased his way back to the rental and sent Champagne a text, letting her know the police were there and he was still outside if she could get away somehow. Then he waited and watched the side door just in case she came out of it.

CHAPTER 8

From her hiding place, Champagne could hear Scrap's footsteps on the colorful tiled floor. Other than that, it was painfully quiet. She swallowed her fear enough to peek over the bar. Champagne saw Scrap pacing in a tight circle between the counter and the bodies. He carefully avoided stepping in a growing pool of blood. When Scrap looked up from the floor, he saw her tear-filled eyes staring back at him.

"Champ, I didn't have a choice. You see they was gonna do something to me. They was tryin' to set me up and shit," he told her with an even more crazed look in his eyes and sweating profusely.

Suddenly, he pointed the gun at Man-Man's corpse and angrily pulled the trigger and repeatedly yelled: "Punk-ass bitch, you set me up! You, you, you!"

The gun was empty, so the boom Champagne braced herself for never came. She stood up, afraid to make eye contact with him again, but she could not help stare as he went through the dead men's pockets.

"Scrap! Scrap, what you doing? Stop it! Stop it!" she said, coming from behind the counter as he removed their keys. "What you finna do?" she demanded, unknowingly standing next to

Big Tone's fallen gun.

"Champ, ya know I gotta find that money and shit before Murdah gets here," he said as he spotted the gun at her feet. "Kick that over here and stay right there."

"Why?" she said as she looked where he was pointing at the empty gun. Afraid to disobey him, she did as told. "Scrap, what you finna do? I won't say nothing. I won't say shit to nobody!" she pleaded.

"Huh? Champ, you trippin' right now. I need you to help me find this shit. Once we got that, we good."

"How are we good when you just killed them, Scrap?"

"Don't nobody know that but us, and you just said you won't say shit. I know I won't." He smiled nefariously.

Champagne dropped her head while trying not to set him off again. In her peripheral vision, she saw a squad car pull into view on the parking lot surveillance monitor behind the bar. She quickly informed Scrap, who rushed to see for himself.

"What we gonna do now? I don't wanna go to jail," Champagne said on the verge of hysteria.

"Fuck!" Scrap said, looking back and forth between the bodies and the monitor. "Turn on the jukebox and stall them as long as you can.

They're just being nosey. If they knew something, there would be more of 'em."

Champagne did as she was told. Since she did not have money for the jukebox, she pressed Autoplay on the club's DJ equipment, which filled the air with loud, hard-pounding bass. Then she watched as Scrap struggled to drag the bodies into one of the private rooms. She did not want to touch the bodies or blood, but she knew if she did not help him she would go to jail with him. She ran and grabbed all the rags from behind the bar, threw a few on the floor, and then started mopping up the trails of blood with her foot the best she could.

"What now?" she asked when the officer

started banging on the door.

"Calm down and go answer the damn door. Calm the fuck down first, 'cause they gonna get on some bullshit if they see you like that!" he warned her, clearly hearing the fear in her shaky voice.

Champagne took slow, deep breaths all the way to the intercom next to the front entrance.

"Who is it?" she asked, trying to sound as cool as she could.

"It's the police. Could you open the door, please?"

"Just a sec, I gotta get the key. But we're closed for the night, so can you tell me what you're here for?" she responded, trying to stall them so Scrap could finish picking up the knocked over tables and chairs.

Scrap noticed that he had blood on his shirt from hiding the blood-stained towels and moving the bodies. He pulled it off, knowing the stains would be hard to see on the black undershirt he was wearing.

"Open the door, and then we can talk."

Scrap grabbed Champagne's arm.

"Don't try no dumb shit. Remember your friend downstairs," he warned, sounding even more like a maniac than before. She nodded, and he turned away from her while still trying to clean the blood off his hands with the shirt.

"You gotta wet it," she told him before she

opened the door enough to peek out. "What's the problem?" she asked the officers.

"We're following up on a Shotspotter report in the area, and a few of your neighbors pointed us in this direction," the young rookie cop explained.

"Who else is inside with you?" the older officer asked, after seeing Scrap's shadow moving around on the floor.

"Ummm, my boyfriend. I mean, the owner."

"Which one is it?" he inquired, picking up her nervousness. "My boyfriend is the owner, sir," she answered, giving them her best smile.

"Let us have a talk with him," the older cop said, pushing his way into the loud club. "Hey!"

he yelled to get Scrap's attention over the pounding bass.

Scrap had just stuffed his bloody shirt in a box behind the DJ booth when the first officer came into view.

"What's up, Officer? Is there a problem, or y'all just stopping in for a drink? As you see, I'm closed for the night."

"That's a little loud. Turn it down, please," the officer said while looking Scrap up and down.

As soon as Scrap paused the song, the rookie took his eyes off Champagne's butt long enough to spot the gun that Scrap had left lying on the bar when he traded it for Big Tone's loaded one.

"Bill! Gun!" he yelled, causing his partner to take his eyes away from Scrap a moment too long.

Without a bit of hesitation, the older cop reached for his gun, but the crazed man was fast. Scrap snatched out his gun from behind his back, stuffed in his pants, and shot the officer closest to him three times in the body. Before the cop's body could hit the floor, Scrap was firing at the rookie.

Both the officer and Champagne dove to the floor. The cop was hit in the thigh, but he was still able to return fire. When he screamed out in pain, Scrap ran up on him and squeezed off shots in his direction. Champagne slid back behind the bar. She screamed when she looked back and saw the rookie's head violently snap to the side.

"Shut the fuck up! Shut up so I can think!" Scrap snapped at her.

A few moments of silence was all they had before the older cop started moaning in pain. Realizing that the cop had on a vest, Scrap stomped over to the fallen officer and shot him in the head as well.

"No, no, no!" Champagne cried.

"Shut the fuck up, bitch, and go make sure the door is locked. And don't try nothing," he commanded while waving the gun at her.

"Okay, okay! Don't shoot me," she pleaded,

holding her hands out in front of her in fear.

"What?" he questioned, when he noticed what he was doing. "Just lock the damn door," he demanded while lowering the gun. He began to pace again trying to figure out his next move. "Come on! Go downstairs and get our shit so we can get the fuck outta here."

He did not wait for her to answer. He just grabbed her arm and practically dragged Champagne through the club down to his office. She knew it was best not to try to fight him, but still feared what he would do to her friend if she did not do something. So fell to the floor and pretended to twist her ankle to slow him down. She hoped to use his feelings for her against him and make him forget about Playthang.

* * *

Playthang ran until she could not run anymore. She then found a junkyard in which to hide and rest while still feeling a bit dizzy from the beating and loss of blood.

The old hoarder who lived in the house looked out her kitchen window and saw something that did not belong. At first glance she thought it was someone trying to steal her goods, but then she noticed the person was not moving. She grabbed a thick iron pipe by the door and went out to have a closer look. She found a passed out and bloodied Playthang clutching a large duffle bag. When she could not wake Playthang up, she grabbed the bag and took it into the house to try to find some form of identification. Inside the bag she found a cell phone, a large amount of money, and drugs. The old woman removed the phone and then put the bag underneath the kitchen sink before dialing 9-1-1.

When the paramedics got there, they placed Playthang on a gurney and then loaded her into the ambulance. Even though the woman did not know anything about the man she found dressed like a woman in her yard, she still rode in the back of the ambulance with Playthang to the nearest hospital emergency room.

CHAPTER 9

Concealed by the shadows in the interior of the rental, Max waited for the right time to move. He sat up in the seat when he saw the door open for the officers to enter Bonkerz. He picked up the gun from his lap and made up his mind to run in the side entrance as soon as the police walked out the front door. As he moved into position, he heard another round of gunshots break out inside. Again he froze. Max could not believe the gunfight he was hearing.

"Shit, shit, Champ! Let a nigga know what the fuck's going on! Something!" he said to himself.

That was when he realized he forgot his phone in the van and turned back to get it. By the time he retrieved his phone, Scrap and Champagne were rushing out of the side door. This time Max left his phone on purpose and crept up on the two as they headed toward Badman's Audi. He slowed when he was close enough to hear them talking. Max did not want to rush in, because he did not know where the police officers were; and the furthest thing from his mind was them lying dead inside the club. He also noticed Champagne walking with a slight limp as Scrap held on to her arm with one hand, a gun in the other.

"What are ya doing, Scrap? Let's just go.

Let's get outta here. She's probably telling the police what you did to her right now and think about what you just did."

"Just shut the fuck up and look out for me while I search this nigga's car for the rest of the money. We really need it now."

"We don't need shit! You do. I ain't done shit, and I ain't helping you. Just let me go and run. I won't say shit to nobody."

"Bitch, you think I did all this shit tonight and I'ma just let you go? You stupid. They gonna be lookin' for the both of us when they find them dead cops. Now shut the fuck up before I knock you the fuck out!" Scrap threatened Champagne before he opened the trunk of the car.

Max was pressed against the building. He

could see Champagne was afraid and after hearing the threats, he knew she was not trying to set him up for her man. Max saw how she was looking around the dimly lit parking lot undoubtedly searching for him. It was good that she did not see him so she would not spoil his surprise attack as he inched closer. He also did not want to give Scrap the chance to use Champagne as a shield when he drew down on him. By the time Champagne noticed Max, he was only a few feet away. He threw his hands up to silence her so he could get all the way up on Scrap, who was bent over deep in the trunk.

When Scrap stood up after he found the backpack of cash stashed behind the sub box, Max jumped him from behind. He punched him with a hard right cross and then locked his arms around him and tried to slam Scrap to the ground, but he was stronger than Max thought. Scrap dropped his weight, spun around, and headbutted him in the face, just hard enough to cause Max to loosen his grip. Just as quickly, Scrap then put him in a headlock.

"Bitch-ass nigga. It ain't sweet!" he yelled into Max's ear as he applied pressure.

Max did his best to break free of the powerful chokehold. He could not breathe, and Scrap was still adding pressure to the point that Max thought he would break his neck. Max passed out, and Scrap let him drop to the ground.

"Champ! Champagne! Stop and come back here!" he yelled behind her as she ran with the bag of money. Seeing that she was not going to stop, he picked up his gun from the trunk and fired a shot over her head. "Bitch, I said stop!"

She screamed and dropped to the ground.

"Please don't! Don't shoot me!" Champagne begged while covering her head with her hands.

"Get the fuck over here!" he commanded as he jogged toward her. "So you was just gonna leave me, huh, Champ?"

"No! Wait! What else was I supposed to do? He had a gun and I was scared," she explained. The way Scrap was acting told her that he did not recognize Max. "Who is that anyway? Did you kill him?" Champagne asked, now hearing police sirens in the distance.

"I don't know, maybe one of them niggas.

Fuck him! Let's get the fuck outta here before the cops get here," he answered, taking the bag from her and tossing it over his shoulder.

He then took her by the arm and pushed her toward his car.

Champagne fought the urge to break free and run toward the busy street. She did not fight him, knowing that it was best to play along if she wanted to survive. Her heart hurt for Max, but she fought back the pain. Once in the car, Scrap sped past where he was lying on the ground, and she stole a glance that caught Max struggling to get up off the ground. Now Champagne fought the urge to scream out in joy, hiding her smile by staring out the passenger window. She was happy that both of her friends were alive, and all she had to do was stay that way. She knew she still needed help to get away from Scrap, so she made plans to text Max and let him know where Scrap had taken her as soon as she could. Scrap had not searched her, and she still had her phone hidden in her back pocket.

* * *

Max sat up against the bumper of the Audi, trying to regain his bearings after being choked out. He heard the police sirens blaring and got to his feet. That was when he saw their flashers light up the night as they raced through the street on the next block over. He did not know if they were coming where he was or not, and he was not going to risk sticking around to find out with a gun on him and two possible dead cops not far from him.

Max's legs were still a little unsteady, and the police were too close to try to make it to the rental, so he scooped up the keys that Scrap dropped to the Audi, got inside, and raced out of the parking lot. As he reached the end of the block, a squad car sped around the corner and smashed head-on into him. Max quickly shook it off and jumped from the car. He ran as fast as he could back in the direction of Bonkerz away from the accident. Max knew he would not make it on foot, so he had to make it to the rental. He dove to the ground as cop cars raced by him toward the crash. When he was safely inside the van, he took a few breaths to calm himself and then backed out of the other end of the alley. As Max spun the van around, he paused long enough to see an ambulance joining the crowd of cop cars in Bonkerz's lot.

Max drove off and then picked up the phone and texted Champagne asking if she was okay and where she was. Max looked at his gloved hands and was glad he had not left his prints in the Audi. But at the stoplight, he noticed blood on his shirt, and for the first time, he realized that his head was bleeding. He knew he was in serious trouble if the police found the blood in the Audi. Max knew he needed a cover story, so he did what he was told to do in times like this. He called Tia and asked her to meet him at his place.

CHAPTER 10

From her surroundings and the direction in which they were heading, Champagne guessed Scrap was taking her to his lakefront condo instead of his place on the east side. She continued ignoring his ranting by thinking of how to get the time alone she needed to get in touch with Max.

"Damn. Fuck! The police are coming."

"What?" she asked, using the side mirror to look behind them.

The two of them watched the squad car weave its way through the traffic behind them.

The cop turned on the squad car lights once he caught up to them. The flashing lights made both of their hearts skip. Scrap knew he was only a couple of blocks away from the entrance of his building's parking garage, which was too close for him to try to lose them. So he slowed down while looking for a place to pull over, hoping he could talk his way through whatever reason they had for stopping them.

"Don't say shit! Not a muthafuckin' word."

"What if they ask me somethin'?" she asked before she noticed him picking up his gun from under his leg and pointing it into the car door where he suspected the officer would stand.

She knew from earlier that he did not care

about killing a cop, and if that was his plan, she did not want to be shot in the crossfire. So, she sat back in her seat and watched the squad car through her mirror. Suddenly, its siren blared, but instead of stopping them, the cop took off and flew by them.

"Thank you," Scrap mumbled as he released the breath he was unknowingly holding and then slowly pulled back into traffic.

They drove the rest of the way in silence. Champagne could see he was really stressing over what he had done. Once they were in the safety of his home, his mood was less angry. Champagne knew all she had to do was keep him relaxed.

"I bet he got that shit at his crib," he blurted out, breaking her train of thought.

"Who got what? What are you talking about?"

"The money and shit from the robbery. It's gotta be at Bad's crib. That's the only place where that nigga would trust leaving it," he explained, wiping his sweaty face with the end of his shirt and smearing blood. "Yeah, yeah! Let's go."

"Whoa, Scrap, wait! Ya need to change clothes first 'cause you got blood all over you, and I just need a few moments to get my mind right be before we leave again," she told him, letting her tears fall as she fell into the soft leather chair in which she was standing in front.

"Yeah, you right," he said as he looked at himself in the light and then over at the ugly way the makeup had smeared on Champagne's face from all the crying she had been doing. "Champ, you know I love you, right? I don't wanna hurt you. I fucked up! I know I fucked up bad!" he acknowledged, dropping to his knees and laying his head in her lap.

Champagne did not know what to say. She just rubbed his head for a while before suggesting he should take a quick shower and change clothes before they went to Badman's house in search of things she knew were not there. She was planning to use the time he spent in the shower to escape.

"Yeah, I saw something on television where they used this special light to see blood and gunpowder on clothes. So, we need to change and get rid of our clothes."

"Okay, yeah! You're right. Go turn on the shower for me and wash your face. I'll take you to yo' house so you can change on the way, okay?" Scrap said while standing up. "I'ma be in there in a second. I gotta check my voicemail to see if Murdah or the police tried to call yet."

"Why would the police be calling you?" she asked him as she stood up.

"Because the club is in both of our names, and by now, I know they've tried to get up with them cops they sent. When they find the spot like that, they gonna call one of us. Since I don't know where my phone's at, I gotta check my messages to see how much time we got to get outta town," he explained, walking over to the house phone.

Champagne thought about everything on her way to the bathroom. She knew there was no way Max would be able to get into the building without the doorman knowing. Her best bet was to get Scrap to tell her where Badman's house was so she could tell Max.

She closed the bathroom door behind her and found that it did not lock. She turned on her phone and saw the text from Max, letting her know he had not gotten caught by the police and that he was still there for her. Then her phone was flooded with texts from a few of the girls she worked with at Bonkerz inquiring about the police activity at the club.

"What are you doing in here?" Scrap asked, opening the door and looking in on her. "It's all good so far."

"Nothing, just lookin' at my face," she lied as she hid the phone in a towel she quickly picked up.

"I told you that you needed to wash it," he said, walking toward her and trying to see what was in her hands.

"Let me get in the shower with you. It'll help

me relax some," she said, dropping the towel and pulling her shirt off in front of him to divert his attention from the towel. "Baby, I need you to make me believe it's gonna be alright."

Champagne knew just what to do when she saw the lust in his eyes. She pulled him to her for a kiss. His lips felt nervous and scary at first, and then he put his arms around her. The nervousness melted away, and Scrap felt needy. His heat excited her. She was glad when he took control, leaving her to follow his lead just the way she needed things to go. Once they were undressed, he cupped her breasts as he kissed his way down to them.

For some reason, his touch felt different to

her, almost like it did when she was with a new trick. She pushed the feeling aside as he pushed her breasts together and then licked circles around her nipples, skillfully licking from one nipple to the other. She was enjoying it more than she wanted to, but she would not and could not pull back or stop him if she wanted her plan to work. This was about survival for her, so she gave in to the way he was making her feel.

Champagne dug her nails into his shoulders as she pushed him to his knees. Scrap's kisses walked down her belly while he dragged his hands down her back until they found her butt. When his lips reached her mound, she felt his hot breath on her opening, and she placed her leg over his shoulder. Then with her hand on top of his head, she guided his mouth where she wanted it to be most.

"Yes, yes! Right there, baby. Make me cum. I wanna cum for you, baby," she moaned as Scrap began flicking his tongue across her clit.

Scrap dipped his fingers into her warmth as he worked his tongue, and within moments, she lost control by cumming hard for him. Scrap was too caught up in her to think about anything else. He stood up and spun her around, and Champagne bent over for him. She held on to the sink as his thickness filled her from behind. He was pounding in and out of her wetness fast and hard, holding her tightly by the hips so he could hit it harder and harder. She moaned and screamed while throwing her butt back at him, temporarily forgetting he was a danger to her. As soon as he lost his rhythm, she knew he was about to nut. She stood up, pushed him out of her, and then dropped to her knees and faced him. She took him in her mouth and hands and sucked and jerked him off until he released his load all over her face and chest.

"Fuck, fuck, fuck! That's the police!" he told her when the ringing of the house phone interrupted his bliss.

"How you know? It could be somebody else."

"Don't nobody else call this line but the doorman and the police."

"Answer it so we can know for sure," she told him, knowing it was the opening she needed to respond to Max.

* * *

Tia got dressed after she got off the phone with Max. He told her that he needed her to meet him at his place right away, but he did not tell her what it was about. She knew something was wrong, and to be on the safe side, she took her gun with her as she rushed out to her car.

CHAPTER 11

Sitting in his brightly lit living room, Max explained to Tia what she needed to know about Champagne and why he needed to help her get away from her boyfriend who was holding her hostage. Tia hung on his every word while she tended to the cuts and scrapes that Max received from the car crash.

"Max, do you know how much trouble you're in right now? You will go to prison behind this!" she snapped in between blotting a deep cut on his forearm with an alcohol-dipped napkin.

"I know, but not if you help me," he told her,

sounding tired and humble as he tried to deal with the sting of the alcohol.

"How in the hell do you think I can do that, and why do you think I would?" she asked, pressing harder than ever on the cut with the napkin.

"Whoa, ease up, Tia! Damn. I'm askin' you. A nigga's tellin' you I need you, and if you didn't care, ya wouldn't still be here or you'd be lockin' me up yourself right now," Max said as he grabbed her hand. "Tia, please?" he begged while looking into her angry eyes.

Before she could give in to him, someone started knocking on the door.

"I thought you said your people didn't knock on your door?"

"They don't. I don't know who the fuck that is. It might be the police comin' about that crash," he whispered.

"No, they don't work that fast, but you should go in your room just in case," she said as she stood with him. "I'll see who it is." She then walked over to the door. "Who is it?" Tia asked once Max was out of sight.

"Is Max here?" a female voice asked, sparking Tia's curiosity. She quickly opened the door. "And who are you?" she demanded, looking up and down at the woman.

"Tell him it's Kake and it's important," Kake replied, matching her attitude.

Max emerged from the bedroom when he heard Kake's voice. He was relived it was not the police but upset by Kake's timing.

"Kake what's so? Fuck it, what?" he asked, trying to check his anger.

"I went to the club, and it was surrounded by police and shit. So, I tried to call you, but yo' phone keeps going straight to voicemail," Kake told him, pushing her way past Tia into the apartment. "I know you be up in there, so when you didn't answer, I had to see if you was good. What happened to yo' face?" she asked once she got a good look at him.

"I was in a car accident, but I'm good," he answered as he walked over to check his phone. "Shit! My battery's dead," he told them, putting it on the charger on the kitchen counter.

"Now who is she to you, Max?" Tia

demanded while marching over and snatching the phone out of his hand to be sure she had his full attention.

She tossed the phone down and tried her best to let Kake know that she was more than a friend to him.

"Look here, Tia, I don't got time for this shit. I was messing with Kake before we got together, but it wasn't like what we have," he said as he looked over at Kake. "And you can lose yo' attitude, Kake. Ya know what it is!"

"I don't got an attitude, Max. She's the one actin' like a punk bitch about shit. Ya know I'm with whatever you with, daddy. I'm sorry I didn't call, but I was worried about you. I didn't know if you needed me to bail you out of jail or what. So don't be mad at me."

"Bitch, who you callin' a punk bitch? I'll drag yo' fat ass, hoe!" Tia snapped at Kake.

"Hey, hey, hey! I heard something next door, I think," Max said, but the two were too busy going back and forth with threats to hear him. "I said shut the fuck up, so I can hear!" he yelled.

* * *

Scrap slid down into the passenger seat of his Escalade just before Champagne pulled it to a stop in front of Badman's house. Just as it was planned, she walked up to the front door dressed in one of Scrap's oversized hoodies and heels. She rang the doorbell a few times as well as banged on the door to be sure the place was empty. When no one answered, she waved to let Scrap know the coast was clear.

Scrap instantaneously hopped out of the truck carrying a large flathead screwdriver. Once he got on the porch, he told Champagne to keep watch while he broke into the house by jamming the tool between the lock and door. He had to repeat the process four times before the lock gave way. Once they were inside, they went right to work searching for the money and drugs that Champagne knew were not there. After almost an hour of destroying the place, all they found was a bit more than $10,000 and a little under two kilos of crack hidden in the cushions of the cheap sofa.

"Fuck this bitch-ass nigga!" Scrap yelled, standing in the middle of the trashed front room.

"Where the hell did he hide it?"

Champagne skittishly stood off to the side holding the cash and drugs, silently watching him looking around the place that they had ransacked. She could see he was slipping back into his panic mood.

"Bae! Baby! Let's get outta here before we get caught. There ain't nowhere else to look. We got this stuff here, so let's go," she pleaded with him, taking a few timid steps closer to him.

"Fuck this lil' shit!" he exploded, snatching one of the bags of crack from her hands and slamming it into the far wall. "I need my fuckin' real money, not that petty shit!"

Champagne jumped back thinking he might hit her.

"Yeah, I know, but it's not here. Scrap, he could've put that shit anywhere. You know he knows ya knew where this house was, so he could've got a new spot that ya don't know about. Whatever, but we've spent too much time in here already. We need to get the fuck outta here before we get caught," she explained as she pulled him by the arm toward the door.

"Yeah, you're right. Let's go," he agreed as he took her hand and they ran back out to the truck and pulled off. "I need to get someplace to think of a way to get out of this mess."

"My house. Take me to my house. Won't nobody be lookin' for you over there. And I need to put on somethin' and get outta these heels," she told him, pulling off one of her shoes to

143

encourage him.

* * *

Champagne's cell phone had been vibrating almost the entire ride to her place. She prayed it was Max, so she could let him know that she was at home. She hated that Scrap did not park in back so she could see if Max was home. But with Scrap so close to his breaking point, Champagne knew it would not be hard to convince him stay at her place until Max made it back.

"Champ, pack some clothes. We're going to visit my family in Chicago. That way I'll have you and them to say I wasn't in town when the police call."

"What did you tell 'em the last time?"

"Nothing. That was just the security letting me know the police was at the club."

"Okay, well how are you gonna explain answering the phone at yo' condo?" she asked, watching him lie back on her sofa.

"I got a burner phone in the truck. I'll just forward the line to it. I got this, so just get ready to go."

"Okay, I'll change and pack an overnight. You should try to rest some so you won't be too tired driving," she suggested before she disappeared into her bedroom and closed the door behind her.

"Just don't take all night!" he told her before he lit half a blunt that was in the ashtray on the coffee table.

It surprised Champagne to see the missed calls were from Scrap's number. She wondered if it was the police. Just as she was about to read the text from Max, the number called again, and she accidentally answered it.

"Hello! Hello, Champ?"

"Who is this?" she asked, unable to make out the muffled voice. "It's me, girl. Where you at? I've been trying to call you. Are you okay?"

"Oh my God, Play! Where you at?"

"I'm in the hospital. When I escaped, I just ran until I passed out in this lady's yard. She found me and brought me here," Playthang explained while looking at the nice woman sitting across from her watching the news.

"Oh my God! Is you okay?"

"I'm a little beat up, but I'll live. I was just so scared for you. Are you still with him?"

"Yeah, we at my house right now. But his crazy ass is tryin' to make me go to Chicago with him."

"No, you gotta get the fuck away from him!"

"I know. His crazy ass killed Bad and some police."

"What!" Playthang cut her off. "You need to get away from him now before he kills you. Champ, try to get to my house. When I left, I took all his shit. My friend here took it and put it up for me. I'm trying to get them to let me leave, but if they don't, I'm just gonna walk out. You just—!"

Scrap suddenly barged into the room, and

Champagne hung up and tried to hide the phone under her thigh.

"Who the fuck was you talkin' to?" he demanded, rushing up and grabbing her by the throat.

Fearing for her life made Champagne fight back. She tried to kick him between the legs, but she missed both times. Scrap picked her up by the throat and then slammed her hard to the floor.

"Scrap, stop!" she yelled before he hit her with his fist. "Stop, I'm sorry, baby. I didn't mean to kick you. You just scared me!" she pleaded while shielding her head with her arms.

"Who the fuck was that, Champ? Who was you on the phone with?" he yelled. Champagne saw his fist was ready to beat her face in. "Play. It was Playthang!"

"What?" he asked as he let go of her and picked up the phone. "Does that bitch got my shit?" Scrap asked, putting his foot onto her chest so she could not get up. "Let's see if we can make a trade for yo' ass," he said as he redialed the number.

CHAPTER 12

The sudden way Champagne disconnected the call alarmed Playthang. It made her worry more about her friend alone in the hands of the crazy man.

"Hey, is everything okay?"

"I don't know. I'm not sure what just happened. She just hung up, and I don't wanna call back if he's in the room with her," Playthang explained to Jan as she stood up from the bed.

"No, don't do that. If that muthafucka is as crazy as you say, he might hurt her like he did you."

After a few moments, the phone rang with Champagne's photo on the screen. Playthang answered it by reflex.

"Champ, what happened?"

"Shut up, bitch, and listen, and I won't knock this hoe's teeth out!" Scrap threatened, not letting Playthang finish.

"What! Okay, Scrap, just don't hurt her."

"I see you don't know how to listen or is it that ya think it's a game?" he said before he started slapping Champagne a few quick times with his gun while holding the phone so Playthang could hear her screams. "Is there anything else you gotta say?" He did not wait long for an answer. "Good, now if you don't want me to kill this sneaky no-good bitch, tell me where you at so I can come get my shit."

Just to add more fear and panic to the situation, Scrap snatched up a lamp from the nightstand next to the bed and slung it across the room into the wall. He had the phone on speaker so both women could hear everything. When Playthang heard Champagne scream again, that was all it took to agree to what the lunatic wanted.

"Okay! Alright! Meet me at my place. Champ knows where it is. Scrap, if I don't see her with you alive or I see anybody else, you ain't getting shit!" Playthang told him before she hung up in his face to show that she was serious.

Playthang did not want to get the kind old woman hurt, so she did not tell him to meet her at her house.

"Where are my clothes?"

"You're not well enough to leave here. Just call the police and let them get the bastard," Jan said as she helped Playthang get dressed.

"No, I can't call the police. He'll kill her and make them kill him before he gives up."

The phone started playing a different ringtone with the word *Mob* flashing on the screen.

"Who's that?"

"I don't know," Playthang said, picking it up off the bed. "Hello, who is this?"

"This is Murdah. Put fam on the phone."

"Oh shit! Shit!" Playthang cursed, waving the phone in the air like it was hot.

"Who is it?" Jan asked, wondering who else could have Playthang so panicky.

Playthang put a hand up to silence Jan and then made her mind up to tell him what was going on.

"Umm, Mr. Murdah, this is Play, and I work at Bonkerz. Scrap ain't here. I took his phone and stuff when he tried to kill me. He's gone crazy thinkin' everyone's out to get him, and right now he has Champagne hostage somewhere."

"Whoa, shut up! Not on the phone. You the

he-she, right?"

Playthang knew it was not the time to be offended if she wanted to save her friend.

"Yeah."

"Okay! Where you at right now? I'ma come to you, so ya can tell me all that shit. I'm pulling up by the club right now, and it's all bad. On my life, if ya real with me, you ain't got shit to worry about."

Playthang knew Murdah to be a man of his word as well as a killer. She knew if she backed out now, he would not stop looking for her until she was dead.

"Okay, pick me up from St. Mary's Hospital. I'll be outside the ER waiting area, but you gotta hurry 'cause I'm supposed to be going to meet him."

Murdah agreed and ended the call. Playthang then explained the plan to Jan before they slipped out of the hospital room unnoticed by the many nurses that were busily rushing around the halls. She gave Jan instructions to go separate the cash from the rest of the contents and then to put the bag someplace in her yard that was easy to get to, but not easy to see from the alley. She also asked her to hold on to the money until she needed it. Once she was sure Jan understood, she put her in a cab and sent her home. Playthang knew the risk she was taking by trusting a woman she had just met and a vicious crime boss, but she felt she owed it to her friend to take the risk.

Two Ford Explorers, one gray and the other black, turned into the parking lot and stopped beside the entrance where Playthang was pacing as she nervously waited.

"Hey, yo! Get in," the driver of the gray SUV told her.

"Where's Murdah?"

"Get the fuck in. I ain't got time for this punk shit!"

Playthang backed away from the trucks as she pulled out her phone and called Murdah.

"I'm in the truck lookin' right at you. Get in," he told her as soon as he answered. With that said, Playthang got in the back of the gray truck where he was, and the driver pulled off, with the other truck following closely behind them. "Now, tell me what in the fuck is going on with fam."

Playthang told him all she knew, starting from the beginning. She left out the part about the sex game she had played with Scrap, but she made sure to tell him that Champagne was planning to leave Scrap. She laid it on thick so Murdah would believe that was the reason Scrap was acting crazy.

* * *

In the midst of Tia and Kake's non-stop bickering, Max heard the commotion in Champagne's unit and moved closer to the wall to try to hear better.

"Say, stay here. Somebody's in Champ's crib. I think it's them," he told them, putting a halt to their argument.

That's when they heard a crash followed by a woman screaming. Max knew it was Champagne. He grabbed a gun from the table and ran out to investigate. The first thing he noticed when he made it to the front of the house was Scrap's Escalade, which confirmed that he was the one with her. Max crept onto the porch and then pressed his ear to the door. He tried to judge how many others were inside the apartment with them before he rushed in. All he heard was his friend's continuous screams, so he smashed the door in and rushed inside gun first.

He cautiously made his way toward the bedroom where all the pandemonium was coming from.

"Drop it, nigga!" Max ordered Scrap as soon as he entered the room and saw him with a gun in her face.

"Whoa, nigga! You drop it or I'll blow this bitch's mind!" he responded, pressing the gun to her forehead.

Max hesitated as he contemplated whether he should try his luck and take the shot. Scrap must have read his mind, because he suddenly yanked Champagne to her feet and used her for a shield while still holding his gun firmly against her jaw.

"Okay, okay, chill!" Max answered, lowering his weapon as he backed out of the doorway.

"I said drop it!"

"No, don't! He won't kill me," Champagne yelled before she tried to pull away from Scrap. "Look, either squeeze the trigger or get that outta my damn face!"

Max noticed Scrap adjusting his finger on the trigger and the crazed look in his eyes. Max felt that if he did not do as Scrap said, the lunatic might just pull the trigger; and if he did, he would shoot him. He took a few more steps backward until he was in a place he could dive for cover if

Scrap turned the gun on him.

"Max, don't!" she pleaded as she watched him place his gun down on top of one of the surround-sound speakers beside him.

"Look, I did what ya said. Now let her go," Max commanded, dropping his hands to his side and readying himself to dive out of the way.

"Fool-ass nigga. That ain't how it works. Yo' fool ass should've listened to her and got the fuck outta here. Wait! Are you the same nigga from earlier?" Scrap realized as he trained his gun on him. "Y'all muthafuckas in this shit together! Where's my shit?" he questioned as he slapped Champagne with the gun to let Max know he was not playing with them.

"Noooo!" she screamed, unfazed by the blow to the head from the butt of the gun.

Champagne feared he was about to shoot Max, so she stomped on Scrap's foot as hard as she could with her bare foot. She then fought to break free from his grip on her hair.

* * *

Playthang was parked in the alley behind Jan's house and continued to bargain for Murdah's help to save her friend from Scrap.

"Play, you giving me my shit back. The shit ya sayin' makes sense, so there ain't no reason for me not to help. Just give me my shit and tell me where we gotta go. On the mob, that nigga ain't gonna touch neither one of you ever again."

Playthang believed him, but she only gave him back the drugs just in case he tried to go back on his word and left them to fend for themselves with Scrap.

"Here, this everything I took. I think if we leave now we can catch them at Champagne's house 'cause he thinks I'm in a cab."

"Fam, ya know where ol' girl lives, right?" Murdah asked the driver after checking to see what was in the duffel bag.

"Yeah, if she's still on 25th?" the driver asked, lookin' back at Playthang for confirmation.

"Yeah, just please hurry."

CHAPTER 13

When Scrap took his eyes off of Max to try to deal with Champagne, he rushed in and knocked Scrap's gun aside with one hand while handing Scrap a few hard jabs with the other. Scrap was forced to release Champagne to fight back. As soon as she was free, Champagne pushed Scrap with all she had and knocked him off balance. Max quickly drove him backward and slammed Scrap into the wall. Scrap dodged Max's fist, causing him to bury it in the drywall where his head once was. He then tried to headbutt Max in the nose, but he hit him on the side of his face instead. Champagne jumped in and grabbed for Scrap's hand holding the gun and threw blows of her own over Max's back. She got hold of the gun, and Scrap squeezed the trigger.

"Hey, stop it!" Murdah yelled before the slug slammed into the wall next to him and hit one of his men in the shoulder who was standing out on the porch.

Max saw Champagne fall to the floor as she screamed in pain. He let go of Scrap and ran for his gun on top of the speaker. That was when he noticed they were not alone and that Murdah was being pulled back outside the door. Scrap got off two more shots before Max got his weapon and blindly returned fire. His shot was nowhere close to where Scrap was standing.

Before Max could re-aim, someone fired seven rapid shot from the doorway behind him, hitting Scrap all seven times in the chest. Max did not know what was going on, but he quickly turned and took aim at the young goon.

"Who is that?" Max demanded from his position on the floor. "Drop yo' gun, fam, and we can talk about it!" Murdah yelled from behind the man aiming at Max. "Champ, is you good?"

"Champagne, it's me! Murdah, tell yo' guy to put his gun down!" Playthang called out to her.

"No, Play, he's one of them. Get away from them!"

"Champ, we good. Play told me everything," Murdah told her.

"Hey, don't shoot. I'm coming in," Playthang

said, slowly walking in holding her hands where Max could see them. "Oh my God! What did he do to you?"

Playthang ran over to where Champagne was slouched against the stove. Max remembered Playthang from the club and lowered his gun,

"Hey, I'm with her, my nigga. Don't shoot," he informed them as he stood up, so they could see him.

Murdah and his men entered the apartment. They walked straight over to where Scrap was lying dead on the floor and where Playthang was holding Champagne, who was crying near where Max was standing.

"It's all good, fam! We just here to make sure

our girl is good. Play told me how that nigga went crazy. I ain't got no issue with you. But we all need to get the fuck outta here now before the Feds get here," Murdah told them after nudging the body with his foot to see if Scrap was really dead. "Yeah, folks, y'all two get the body and get rid of it," he instructed his men.

"Don't move! Set your guns down slowly and interlock your fingers behind your heads!" Tia ordered from the doorway, with her gun on Murdah and his goons. "Max, is you alright?"

"I don't think so, bitch. You need to put that down before we drop you!"

"Hold on! Wait! She's good," Max announced as he stepped out in front of the goons and Tia, waving his arms for them to lower their guns.

"They came to help, so put yo' gun down so they can do what they gotta do, Tia," he pleaded with her.

"Is he dead?" she asked, seeing Scrap's body for the first time. "He was finna kill us. They got here just in time, but ya gotta let them move the body before the police get here."

"We called them already," Kake informed as she walked up next to Tia. "Oh shit, girl, you gotta let them go. Ya don't know who that is. Just let 'em go!" she pleaded with Tia after she saw Murdah and his men she recognized from Bonkerz.

"Okay, but I can't let you take the body."

"Bitch, what you mean you can't let us take the body?"

"Fam, she's an officer of the state. Just go. I got this. She won't say shit about you," Max told Murdah before he took the gun from Tia to let him know he had her.

"Alright, so how y'all gonna explain this?" Murdah asked.

They could hear the sound of approaching sirens as they all walked out of the apartment. Playthang and Kake helped Champagne, who had broken her already bruised ankle in the tussle with Scrap. Her hand was bleeding badly from the gunshot.

"I got this. Just leave the gun he was shot with and get out of here now, if you're going to go," Tia told him.

"Do what she said, and let's get the fuck

gone," Murdah ordered his men. "Hey, Champ, you and Play need to come see me as soon as ya can," he said before climbing into the back of the gray SUV that smashed off before he could get the door closed good.

Max picked up the gun that the goon dropped on the ground before he got in and raced away. He took his shirt and wiped it down before handing it to Tia.

"I can't be here, Tia. Ya know that," he reminded her, but it was too late for him to make a run for it.

"Don't worry about nothing. I got you," Tia assured him as she pulled out her credentials and held them up with her gun so the cops could see them as they exited their cars and swarmed in.

After Tia explained to the detective what went on, Max was taken into custody and put in the back of a squad car on a probation hold on Tia's orders. It was the best she could do on short notice. Kake was pissed at her for doing so. She promised Max she would do whatever she could to get him out, before storming off. Playthang and Champagne were put in the ambulance and rushed to the nearest hospital. On the way, the two did their best to get their stories together for the rest of the questioning. They told the truth about how Scrap got high and beat Playthang, thinking she was trying to set him up.

Champagne explained how she was beaten

and then taken hostage after she stopped Scrap from killing her friends. She told them that she thought he had killed Max before he took her back to her place to hide out.

Playthang told them how Scrap called her and told her to come over with the stuff he thought they had stolen from him for Champagne's life. She told the officers that she did not have it, but she thought she could save her somehow on her own.

Back at the scene, Tia gave her statement to the detectives for the third time. She told them that she was in the area when she got the call from Max telling her that he needed her help, because he got into a fight with his neighbor's boyfriend. She told them that when she pulled up, she saw another man run off the porch and toss the gun. She said she called for help and then went into the unit to see if there was anyone there that needed her help. Once inside, Playthang showed up with the police not far behind.

"So, Ms. Munday, do you plan on pressing charges on your client?" the detective asked when he had all he needed to know about the events that took place.

"No charges just yet. I'll have to talk it over with my supervisor to see how to handle things, if you don't plan on hitting him with anything."

"I don't see anything he did wrong at this time, but you should hold him until we're done with our investigation."

"That won't be a problem. I plan on making him sit for a bit so he can think about how close he came to going to prison, or worse—losing his life."

Tia went back to lock up Max's unit and found Kake there waiting on her with Max's gun in her hand.

"How could you do that to him? Bitch, you foul!"

"Hold on! Put the gun down and let's talk about this, because it's not what you think," Tia said, holding her hands up and trying not to do anything to make Kake shoot her.

"Bitch, you had him put in jail! How the fuck else am I supposed to see it?"

"Please, just hear me out. I care for Max. I

wouldn't do anything to hurt him. Trust me, Kake, I did what was needed to keep him safe."

"I don't know you, but I know him, and if he got yo' ass around, that means he trusts you too. So I'ma give you the benefit of the doubt. But I want yo' ID so I'll know how to find you if you don't do as ya say," Kake said as she held out her hand and tipped it with the nose of the gun to show Tia there was no negotiating about the ID.

Tia was reluctant to give her address to Kake, but she gave it to her to show that she was a woman of her word.

"Okay, now that we have that understanding, how about we go over what happened tonight. And you can tell me who in the hell those guys were you had me let go. I'm sure I know your relationship with Max, but what is his with Champagne? Please don't insult me by saying she's just someone you work with."

"Well, what's really good with me and Max is for you to ask him when ya get him out. As a woman, I'll admit that I care about him a lot. He's done so much for me. But I'm like you when it comes to Champ. I didn't know he fucked with her like that."

CHAPTER 14

Max sat in the house of correction for three weeks on a hold waiting for Tia's supervisor at the probation office to decide whether or not he should be revoked. Max had only seen Tia once since the night she had him placed into custody.

"I had to do things this way, Max. I know you don't like it; I don't either. But you're only going to be held for twenty-one days, and that's better than them locking you up over that mess at your place."

Even though Tia's explanation for what she

had done made all the sense with the circumstances involved, Max was too upset by it to see her actions as anything other than betrayal. So, he refused to see her any more after that professional visit at the county jail the day before he got shipped back out to the HOC to await judgment.

He had not taken the time to memorize Kake's phone number, nor had he trusted her enough to give her his full name. Max hated not being able to get in contact with her, because she still had his car and owed him for the weed he had fronted her. Just when things were looking all bad for him, he received a postcard with a phone number from his ol' buddy Slugga.

Max was on his way to use the phone, when a fight broke out in the dorm between the east-side and south-side gangsters. The brawl got the whole dorm locked down. No movement, no phones, no nothing. Just cold food and a hard bunk until the higher-ups got to the bottom of it and were sure that everyone understood that they were still in control. A few days into the lockdown, Max overheard a new guy tell someone that Bonkerz had reopened under new management. He said that Murdah had always held a soft spot for Champagne and respected Playthang for keeping it real with him by returning the work that was taken from the club by Scrap. Because Murdah believed in keeping his friends close, he gave them Scrap's share in the club.

Hearing their conversation only added fuel to the anger burning within Max. He worried about his apartment and his vehicles. Max was not worried about losing the unit because he had paid up for four months and still had two to go. The only thing he was really worried about was what was hidden in it. He prayed that Slugga had secured the place and his things.

Later that day, Max received a letter informing him that the probation office was requesting another fourteen-day extension.

"Damn! That's fuckery, fam. Them mutha-fuckas are always waiting for the last minute to do shit like that," the guy in the bunk next to his

said when he heard Max read the letter to his

bunk-mate, Skool.

"Say, Skool, do you know how many times

they can pull this shit?"

"Back when I was on it, they could only get

two, but that's changed now. I could be off, but I

think it's one before they gotta give a nigga an

ATR."

"Man, I ain't trying to sit in no halfway house

or no shit like that. I got too much shit going on.

I wasn't just a nigga in the way out there. I was

making major moves in the streets," Max

boasted.

"I feel you, boss, but if they do come at you

with an alternative to revoke ya, don't be a fool. You better take it. At least you'll be free to move around and make sure all your shit's okay. Hell, if I don't get outta here soon, I'ma lose my truck, and that's my bread and meat, feel me?"

"What kinda truck your hype ass got?"

"My bitch is a '99 Ford F-250, and I hit the horn every now and again. But I get money junking, not doing petty cell phone robberies like your dumb ass."

"What they holding you for, Skool?" Max asked, running interference before they got into a fight and made them lock them down even longer.

"These bitches got me on a $250 fine for

driving. The police did me a solid by not having my truck towed, but if I don't get out soon, the city might tow it anyway for sitting in the same spot too long. Then I'm fucked!"

Before Max could respond, the corrections officer yelled his name again from the desk. Max answered, thinking there was some more mail they forgot to give him.

Pack your shit! They lifted your hold, and somebody will be here in a few to get you," the CO told him.

He did not have to tell Max twice. He jogged back to his bunk, stripped it, and then got Skool and his other bunkie's information. He gave them his word that he would look out for them.

Max promised his bunkie that he would put money on the phone, so he could keep in touch to let him know what was going on with his robbery case. Max told Skool he would pay his bail as soon as he walked out the door. He also told him to look him up when he got out, and he gave both of them his number before he rushed out to the release staging area.

* * *

Playthang helped Champagne move out of her unit and into the condo that Scrap owned. Once the apartment was empty, they locked up and tossed the key in the mailbox for the landlord to find. Champagne never planned on going back to the place for anything, not even her friend Max. This was a new start for her, and she was going to shine like a star for all her haters.

After the police released her and Playthang from questioning the night of the shooting, Playthang took her over to Jan's house and got the money her friend was holding for her. With no place to go, Champagne decided to go to the condo where she had spent a few hard hours with Scrap for the night. Playthang decided to go with her. They split the cash there and talked about their plans of what they were going to do with it. Playthang's plans were still the same. She was going to go and pay the best doctor to make her complete. She needed to be all the woman she knew she was born to be.

* * *

Two weeks later, Champagne and Play-thang were parting ways at the airport. Playthang was on her way to Texas for her sex change.

"Play, are you sure you're gonna be okay? I'll come with you if you need me to," Champagne asked with tears in her eyes.

"Yeah, I'm okay. I'm good. I need you to stay here and get the club back up and running. So, when I do come back, I can make one of them bum-ass bitches suck on my brand-new pussy onstage for all to see." Playthang laughed and did a little happy dance.

Her flight was announced. Playthang hugged Champagne and kissed her passion-ately back.

"I just had to get one more in before he's all gone," Champagne told her before letting her catch her flight.

* * *

Max made good on his promise to pay the old man's bail when they gave him his check for the money they took from him when he was booked. He was now sitting at a stop in the parking lot waiting on Kake to pick him up. He was able to call her with the last bit of power his cell phone had before it shut down on him.

"What the fuck does this bitch want?" Max

asked himself aloud when he spotted Tia's truck turn into the lot and head his way. It stopped in front of him, and Kake lowered the passenger window.

"What you doing with her?" he questioned with surprise.

"Why, nigga, you ain't gonna get in? What you finna do, walk?"

"Max, just get in the damn car! You can't stay mad at me. I got you out with no charges like I promised, didn't I?" Tia yelled over Kake's shoulder from the driver's seat.

Max did not put up a fight. He quickly climbed into the back seat and slammed the door.

"Tia, thanks for getting me out. I just got a

letter about me doing fourteen more days and shit."

"That was Kake's idea. I told her that shit wasn't gonna be funny, but she talked me into it."

"How you two get to be such good buddies and shit?"

"I had to put her ass in place for you, daddy, and then I had to show her why you fuck with me," Kake explained as Tia blushed.

"We got something special planned for you, but if you're gonna just be mad, then we're just gonna have fun without you," Tia told him, catching his eyes in the rear-view mirror.

"I don't believe this shit. Y'all fuckin' around?"

"If that's what you wanna call it, but this only works if you're down."

"Hell yeah, I'm with it! I need to holla at my nigga Slugga right quick to see what's up, but my phone's dead."

"I talked to him already. He's gonna holla at you when we done with you and not before," Kake told him.

"I see y'all just gonna make me chill with y'all, so okay. I'm with it. I don't got shit else to say. Just take me to my crib so I can get changed and make sure my shit is good."

To order books, please fill out the order form below:
To order films please go to www.good2gofilms.com

Name: __ _____

Address:_____

City: _____ State: _____ Zip Code: _____

Phone:_____

Email:_____

Method of Payment: Check   VISA   MASTERCARD

Credit Card#:_ _____

Name as it appears on card: _____

Signature: _____

Item Name	Price	Qty	Amount
48 Hours to Die – Silk White	$14.99		
A Hustler's Dream - Ernest Morris	$14.99		
A Hustler's Dream 2 - Ernest Morris	$14.99		
A Thug's Devotion – J. L. Rose and J. M. McMillon	$14.99		
All Eyes on Tommy Gunz – Warren Holloway	$14.99		
Black Reign – Ernest Morris	$14.99		
Bloody Mayhem Down South – Trayvon Jackson	$14.99		
Bloody Mayhem Down South 2 – Trayvon Jackson	$14.99		
Business Is Business – Silk White	$14.99		
Business Is Business 2 – Silk White	$14.99		
Business Is Business 3 – Silk White	$14.99		
Cash In Cash Out – Assa Raymond Baker	$14.99		
Cash In Cash Out 2 - Assa Raymond Baker	$14.99		
Childhood Sweethearts – Jacob Spears	$14.99		
Childhood Sweethearts 2 – Jacob Spears	$14.99		
Childhood Sweethearts 3 - Jacob Spears	$14.99		
Childhood Sweethearts 4 - Jacob Spears	$14.99		
Connected To The Plug – Dwan Marquis Williams	$14.99		
Connected To The Plug 2 – Dwan Marquis Williams	$14.99		
Connected To The Plug 3 – Dwan Williams	$14.99		
Deadly Reunion – Ernest Morris	$14.99		
Dream's Life – Assa Raymond Baker	$14.99		
Flipping Numbers – Ernest Morris	$14.99		
Flipping Numbers 2 – Ernest Morris	$14.99		
He Loves Me, He Loves You Not - Mychea	$14.99		
He Loves Me, He Loves You Not 2 - Mychea	$14.99		
He Loves Me, He Loves You Not 3 - Mychea	$14.99		

He Loves Me, He Loves You Not 4 – Mychea	$14.99		
He Loves Me, He Loves You Not 5 – Mychea	$14.99		
Lord of My Land – Jay Morrison	$14.99		
Lost and Turned Out – Ernest Morris	$14.99		
Love Hates Violence – De'Wayne Maris	$14.99		
Married To Da Streets – Silk White	$14.99		
M.E.R.C. - Make Every Rep Count Health and Fitness	$14.99		
Money Make Me Cum – Ernest Morris	$14.99		
My Besties – Asia Hill	$14.99		
My Besties 2 – Asia Hill	$14.99		
My Besties 3 – Asia Hill	$14.99		
My Besties 4 – Asia Hill	$14.99		
My Boyfriend's Wife - Mychea	$14.99		
My Boyfriend's Wife 2 – Mychea	$14.99		
My Brothers Envy – J. L. Rose	$14.99		
My Brothers Envy 2 – J. L. Rose	$14.99		
Naughty Housewives – Ernest Morris	$14.99		
Naughty Housewives 2 – Ernest Morris	$14.99		
Naughty Housewives 3 – Ernest Morris	$14.99		
Naughty Housewives 4 – Ernest Morris	$14.99		
Never Be The Same – Silk White	$14.99		
Shades of Revenge – Assa Raymond Baker	$14.99		
Slumped – Jason Brent	$14.99		
Someone's Gonna Get It – Mychea	$14.99		
Stranded – Silk White	$14.99		
Supreme & Justice – Ernest Morris	$14.99		
Supreme & Justice 2 – Ernest Morris	$14.99		
Supreme & Justice 3 – Ernest Morris	$14.99		
Tears of a Hustler - Silk White	$14.99		
Tears of a Hustler 2 - Silk White	$14.99		
Tears of a Hustler 3 - Silk White	$14.99		
Tears of a Hustler 4- Silk White	$14.99		
Tears of a Hustler 5 – Silk White	$14.99		
Tears of a Hustler 6 – Silk White	$14.99		

The Last Love Letter – Warren Holloway	$14.99		
The Last Love Letter 2 – Warren Holloway	$14.99		
The Panty Ripper - Reality Way	$14.99		
The Panty Ripper 3 – Reality Way	$14.99		
The Solution – Jay Morrison	$14.99		
The Teflon Queen – Silk White	$14.99		
The Teflon Queen 2 – Silk White	$14.99		
The Teflon Queen 3 – Silk White	$14.99		
The Teflon Queen 4 – Silk White	$14.99		
The Teflon Queen 5 – Silk White	$14.99		
The Teflon Queen 6 - Silk White	$14.99		
The Vacation – Silk White	$14.99		
Tied To A Boss - J.L. Rose	$14.99		
Tied To A Boss 2 - J.L. Rose	$14.99		
Tied To A Boss 3 - J.L. Rose	$14.99		
Tied To A Boss 4 - J.L. Rose	$14.99		
Tied To A Boss 5 - J.L. Rose	$14.99		
Time Is Money - Silk White	$14.99		
Tomorrow's Not Promised – Robert Torres	$14.99		
Tomorrow's Not Promised 2 – Robert Torres	$14.99		
Two Mask One Heart – Jacob Spears and Trayvon Jackson	$14.99		
Two Mask One Heart 2 – Jacob Spears and Trayvon Jackson	$14.99		
Two Mask One Heart 3 – Jacob Spears and Trayvon Jackson	$14.99		
Wrong Place Wrong Time – Silk White	$14.99		
Young Goonz – Reality Way	$14.99		
Subtotal:			
Tax:			
Shipping (Free) U.S. Media Mail:			
Total:			

Make Checks Payable To:
Good2Go Publishing
7311 W Glass Lane,
Laveen, AZ 85339

CPSIA information can be obtained
at www.ICGtesting.com
Printed in the USA
LVHW051603260319
611891LV00019B/670/P